"I'd like to kiss you, Spring."

Since when had Clay started asking permission? Spring wondered. Then she realized he was awaiting her response. She removed her glasses and leaned toward him.

Their lips had barely touched before his mouth began moving seductively over hers. After what seemed like a blissful eternity, Clay pulled away, gave a low, husky laugh and hugged her with fervent enthusiasm. "You never stop surprising me, Spring Reed. We're going to be so good together."

She swallowed hard. "We're . . . what?"

Cradling her face in his hands, he smiled meltingly at her and kissed her nose. "When we make love, it's going to be the most exquisite, most erotic, most incredible thing that has ever happened to either of us. I can't wait."

"I've told you, Clay. We are *not* going to have an affair."

Flashing his most charming grin, Clay grabbed the hand that was pushing against his chest and kissed her knuckles. "We're already having an affair Spring . . . a love affair."

Gina Wilkins hadn't intended to write the trilogy of the Reed sisters—Summer, Spring and Autumn—when she wrote Summer's story in her first Temptation, *Hero in Disguise*. But the more "Crazy Clay" McEntire popped up there, the more this talented new writer wondered what would happen if flamboyant Clay fell in love with Summer's older, rather conservative sister, Spring. And so *Hero for the Asking*, Gina's second Temptation, was born. "Dressing Clay was lots of fun, too," Gina says. Her family and friends chipped in with advice on outrageous outfits, "some too weird even for Clay."

The story of the third Reed sister, Autumn, will be coming your way in Temptation #204, *Hero by Nature*, in May.

Books by Gina Wilkins

HARLEQUIN TEMPTATION
174—HERO IN DISGUISE

Hero for the Asking

GINA WILKINS

Harlequin Books

TORONTO • NEW YORK • LONDON
AMSTERDAM • PARIS • SYDNEY • HAMBURG
STOCKHOLM • ATHENS • TOKYO • MILAN

For Beth Vaughan,
my mother,
who shared her
love of books with me . . .

And for Sally Hawkes,
Linda Palmer and Deborah Perkins,
supportive friends.

Published April 1988

ISBN 0-373-25298-6

1

"SO WHAT'S THIS older sister of yours like, Summer? Am I going to fall madly in love with her?"

Summer Anderson smiled fondly at the lethally handsome blond male who'd thrown himself on the floor at her feet as she rested in an easy chair in her den. She'd found Clay McEntire on her doorstep when she'd returned home from her college class—not an unusual occurrence at her Sausalito house, where her friends often dropped by unexpectedly on Friday evenings. "Not likely," she told him. "I don't think she's your type."

"Since when do you know my type?" he demanded challengingly, grinning up at her. "So far you've tried to fix me up with about a dozen women, and none of them was my type."

"I had such hopes for you and Autumn," Summer mourned with a dramatic sigh, her eyes sparkling mischievously beneath her heavy fringe of golden-brown bangs. "You were supposed to meet her at my wedding and be knocked right onto your cute tush."

"Autumn is certainly a knockout," Clay agreed solemnly. "I liked her very much."

"You treated her like a kid sister," Summer complained.

"She *is* a kid sister."

Summer sighed gustily. "Mine, not yours, idiot."

"So tell me about Spring. God, those names. What would your parents have done if they'd had a fourth daughter born in December? Anyway, all I know about Spring is that she's an optometrist and she's a couple of years older than you."

Summer laughed. "I've always been glad that my parents stopped with three kids. Can you imagine going through life with the name Winter Reed? Sounds like a flavor of LIFE SAVERS. Anyway, about Spring. First off, she's not a couple of years older than I am. She'll be twenty-seven in two months—her birthday's May 14—and I'll be twenty-six in July. She's very fair—blond hair, violet eyes, English-rose complexion. She's taller than I am, five-seven, and slender. Like a model. She takes after our Scandinavian maternal grandmother."

"Don't any of you sisters look alike?" Clay asked in amusement, remembering Autumn's earthy, auburn-haired, green-eyed beauty. Summer's wholesomely attractive features matched her cheerfully extroverted personality—enormous blue eyes, uptilted nose, golden tan, petite frame. From what Clay had heard of the family, it seemed as if the Reed sisters had inherited entirely different features to match their very individual personalities.

"Not a bit," Summer replied gaily. "As far as personality goes, Spring is hard to describe. She's a little like my Derek in some ways. Serious on the surface but with a lively sense of humor hidden underneath. Hardworking, ambitious, goal oriented. Punctual, conscientious, responsible."

Clay chuckled and shook his golden head as he shifted to a more comfortable position on the plush beige carpet of Summer's den. "She's going to hate me, right?"

"I said she wasn't your type," Summer pointed out. "But, to be perfectly honest with you, I think Spring is bored out of her mind. She's tired of always being responsible and mature, and just itching to do something really crazy for a change. She'd never admit it, of course, but I still believe it's true. I think I'll advise her to have a mad passionate affair while she's visiting me. It would do her a world of good."

Clay held up both hands in a gesture meant to call attention to himself. "Sounds good to me. Where do I sign up?"

Summer laughed. "With Spring."

"I can but try."

"Don't blame me if you get shot down."

He looked affronted. "Why? I'm reasonably attractive and definitely available."

"You're more than reasonably attractive and you know it, you gorgeous hunk," Summer teased. "But let's face it, Clay. Spring is going to take one look at those clothes of yours and shudder. You won't get to say a word."

"What's wrong with my clothes?" Clay demanded, shoving himself to his feet and looking down at his lean, six-foot-four length. He wore an unbuttoned purple-yellow-and-white-printed cotton shirt over a yellow T-shirt and baggy white pleated pants. A purple print bandana was knotted around his neck. His sockless feet were tied into bright yellow Reeboks with green laces in the left shoe and red in the right. For Clay, he was actually dressed quite conservatively.

"You don't really want me to answer that."

"Oh, well." He dismissed her criticism with an indolent shrug. "Just remember to tell your lovely sister that I'm willing if she decides to take you up on your advice to have a mad passionate affair. Satisfaction guaranteed."

"Oh, the ego of the man," Summer murmured, her eyes turned toward the ceiling.

"Just stating the facts, ma'am," he drawled.

Summer shook her head sadly. "When it comes right down to it, I'll have to step in and protect her from you, anyway. What I really want is to get her fixed up permanently. You know what they say about us happily married women. We can't stand it until all our friends are suitably wed."

"You'll just have to limit your matchmaking to your sisters. No woman's going to want to find herself married to me."

"Now you're going to hide again behind all those poor troubled kids you work with," Summer muttered with an audible sigh of disgust.

"It's the truth, Summer," Clay protested, more seriously than before. "You know those kids take all my time."

"Hey, don't I work with the same kids? I give many hours to Halloran House, and I'm planning to work at it full-time when I finish my degree, but that doesn't mean I have to sacrifice time with my husband or the family he and I plan to have. Face it, Clay, your work is a very convenient excuse to keep you from committing yourself. You could make some adjustments if you tried. You just haven't found a woman yet who made you want to compromise."

"Summer!" a woman's voice called out from the doorway. "Oh, hi, Clay. Is Spring here yet? We can't wait to meet her."

"No, not yet. She and Derek should be here any minute," Summer answered, rising to greet the couple who'd just entered her den. Derek's sister, Connie, with her bright, improbably red hair and brilliantly toned trendy clothing, made an interesting contrast to the conservatively dressed man at her side, but one had only to look at them to know that Connie Anderson and Joel Tanner were very much in love. The hefty diamond engagement ring on Connie's left hand was further evidence of their commitment.

Clay watched Summer and Connie with a fond smile. He'd known Summer since she'd moved to San Francisco from Arkansas over two years earlier. He'd met Connie when she and Summer had shared an apartment in San Francisco while both of the attractive young women were unattached and dedicated to serious partying when they weren't working at their mutual place of employment. Clay loved them both but had never considered himself *in* love with either. He wondered why.

Even as he joined the conversation around him, he found himself thinking about what Summer had said just before Connie and Joel had entered the room. She'd accused him of using his work with troubled teenagers as an excuse to avoid commitment. He wondered for a moment if she was right, then hastily denied the suggestion to himself. There was no question in his mind that his dedication to the kids was genuine and demanding. He wasn't using that as an excuse . . . was he?

Of course, Summer had been right about one thing. He had never found a woman who made him want to try to change the way his life was now. And it wasn't for lack of trying. At thirty-four, almost thirty-five, Clay experienced the usual healthy desires for a wife and family. He loved children, would like to have one or two of his own. *Could* he make time in his life for a family if he found the right woman?

"So, Clay, how's it going?"

Shaking off his atypical self-scrutiny, Clay grinned at Joel and threw an arm across the other man's shoulders. "Joel, my friend, have I mentioned that we're having a fund-raising drive at Halloran House this week?"

Joel and Clay were almost exactly the same height and age and made a striking picture for the woman who stood in the doorway, looking around in bewilderment. Spring Reed blinked through the glasses perched on her nose at the number of people in the room where she'd expected to find only her sister. Then she stared in feminine appreciation at the two men directly across from her. Both of them were extraordinarily handsome. One was dark-haired, blue-eyed, with a gleam of white teeth beneath a silky dark mustache. But it was the other who made Spring's pulse do an odd little skip and jump.

He was gorgeous. She could think of no other word for him. Thick, slightly shaggy golden-blond hair, classic features and a smile that could easily grace the cover of a popular magazine—*GQ* and *Esquire* came immediately to her mind. The slim but well-developed build of an athlete—baseball, she thought, or perhaps tennis. Then she noted his clothing, her disapproving gaze lingering on his mismatched shoelaces. *One of Summer's oddball friends*, she thought, almost smiling as she tried to picture her ex-boyfriend Roger in such strange attire. Of course, to Roger, leaving off one's tie was ultracasual.

California, she thought wryly, acknowledging a faint twinge of culture shock as she looked away from the colorfully dressed man to find her sister talking to a beautiful woman with copper-red hair and a beaming expression. Her brother-in-law, Derek, placed a hand lightly in the middle of Spring's back, as if sensing her sudden attack of shyness, and she gave him a grateful smile.

An unexpected illness had prevented her from attending her sister's wedding five months earlier, so Spring hadn't met Derek until he'd picked her up at San Francisco International Airport less than an hour before. He had proven to be a little different than what she had expected. The photographs she'd seen had faithfully recorded his almost militarily short tobacco-brown hair, pewter-gray eyes that peered so intensely through dark-rimmed glasses, hard, rugged good looks. But film hadn't been able to capture the almost palpable strength that radiated from Derek Anderson's firm, lean body, nor the hint of the predator beneath the veneer of a civilized businessman.

Spring had been startled to learn that her free-spirited, nonconformist, twenty-five-year-old sister had married a respectable, seemingly average, thirty-seven-year-old management consultant. Now she suspected that there was more to Derek Anderson than met the eye—something that her perceptive sister must have noticed from the beginning. With Derek close behind her Spring moved to greet her sister, whom she hadn't seen in almost eighteen months.

Clay felt Spring's eyes on him from the moment she appeared in the doorway. He looked up and froze, forgetting Joel, forgetting his own name. It wasn't that she was the most beautiful woman he'd ever seen, though she was striking. Pretty, he thought. The word fit her perfectly. Silvery-blond hair, fine as swan's down, pinned into a loose knot on the top of her head with soft little tendrils escaping all around. Light-framed glasses perched on a short, straight nose. Through the glasses he could see her eyes—slightly almond shaped, appearing almost purple from where he stood. Her face was delicately rounded, her mouth seductively painted with a color that fell somewhere between pink and coral. A heather-pink suit clung lovingly to her beautiful body.

Spring, he thought. Yes, the name suited.

He watched her eyes widen as they met his, pleased to sense an answering attraction there. Then he saw her gaze drop to his clothes. He narrowed his eyes, wondering if he'd imagined a slight curl to her lips.

Oh, great, Clay thought ruefully, watching Derek leading her across the room to be warmly welcomed by her sister. *The most fascinating woman I've seen in ages and she turns out to be a snob.* Summer had told him that her sister was rather conservative, but he'd assumed she'd exaggerated. How could free-spirited, warmly accepting Summer be related to a woman who seemed so opposite? He wondered how long it would be until he had the opportunity to confirm his first impression, and found himself hoping he was wrong about Spring.

Spring extricated herself from her sister's enthusiastic hug and smiled into Summer's eyes. "You look so happy!" she remarked with pleasure. She couldn't remember ever seeing such a look of contentment on Summer's face, though Summer had always been one to relish life. Even before the accident over five years earlier that had left her with a permanent limp from a shattered kneecap, Summer had never looked happier to Spring than she did now. "Marriage definitely agrees with you."

"Yes, it does," Summer agreed. "Are you surprised?"

Spring only smiled.

Summer turned to the attractive redhead standing just behind her. "Spring, I want you to meet Connie."

Before Spring could do more than exchange greetings with Summer's best friend and former roommate, the gorgeous blond male she'd noticed a few moments earlier stepped close to her side. Too close, she thought, wondering why she was suddenly having trouble with her breathing. She moistened her lower lip as she smiled tentatively at him.

"So you're Summer's sister," he began in a silky voice, his blue-green eyes glinting with an expression she couldn't begin to read. He offered her his hand and gave her a smile that made her toes curl. "That's a very nice suit you're wearing, but how do you keep from choking with your blouse buttoned up to your throat that way?"

Summer groaned audibly.

"I'm Clay McEntire," the man went on, clinging to Spring's hand and ignoring Summer. "Affectionately known to our little circle of friends as 'Crazy Clay.' I can't imagine where they came up with such a nickname, but you know how those things tend to stay with you. Do you have any nicknames?"

Spring cleared her throat and tugged lightly at her hand, wondering what the man was doing. Why did she have the feeling that he was testing her in some way? What sort of reaction was he hoping to evoke from her? She thought longingly of Little Rock, where people just said "Hello" or "Nice to meet you." She'd just *known* she'd be out of place in proudly unpredictable California!

As the others smiled with fond indulgence at Clay, Spring gave him a cool smile and fibbed that it was nice to meet him, deciding to ignore his question about nicknames. She pulled a little harder at her hand, noting that his hold was anything but light. Definitely a tennis grip, she decided, hoping he couldn't feel her rapid pulse in her fingers.

"Would you like to go outside with me?" Clay offered in a low, suggestive voice. "I could show you the pool."

"I think I'll wait until later, thank you," Spring answered, wishing again that she was back in Little Rock. Who was this guy, anyway? Her eyes turned toward Summer, pleading for help.

"Later is fine," Clay said cheerfully. "Just let me know when you're ready."

"Clay, stop manhandling my sister and behave yourself," Summer scolded, interceding with a light laugh. She reached to firmly pull Spring's hand out of Clay's grasp. "Ignore him, Spring. The rest of us do."

It sounded like good advice, but Spring had a feeling that Clay McEntire was going to be hard to ignore. He was still standing so close to her that she could almost feel the heat radiating from his very nice body. She tried hard to convince herself that he was not igniting an answering flame in her.

Then she was introduced to Joel, who turned out to be Connie's fiancé, and she was relieved when he seemed perfectly normal. Thank goodness he wasn't another screwball like Clay!

"It's very nice to meet you, Spring," Joel greeted her in his pleasantly soft voice. "Everyone was disappointed when you couldn't come to California with the rest of your family for the wedding."

"Not half as disappointed as I was," Spring answered truthfully. Summer and Derek had graciously offered to postpone the wedding when Spring had become ill, but she had refused to allow it. She had no intention of ever letting anyone know that she'd cried herself to sleep on the night of the wedding, lying in her Little Rock apartment, lonely, feverish and ill.

Summer giggled. "I'm sorry," she told her sister, no regret evident in her voice. "I shouldn't laugh at you for being sick—but chicken pox! At your age!"

Spring sighed in resignation. She had expected this. "I knew you found the whole thing hysterically funny— that I missed catching chicken pox in school when you and Autumn had them, then caught them from one of my patients at the age of twenty-six. I'm sure you were sorry that I couldn't come to your wedding, but don't tell me you didn't have a laugh at my expense."

"We all know that your sister has a rather warped sense of humor," Derek murmured straight-faced, his eyes gleaming at his adored wife.

"Definitely warped," Spring agreed in amusement. She had liked her brother-in-law from the moment she'd met him at the airport. She knew now that she was going to love him like the big brother she'd always wanted.

"So, Summer, what's for dinner?" Connie asked brightly.

Summer looked at Connie with a teasingly lifted eyebrow. "Funny, I don't remember asking you to dinner."

"Oh, let her and Joel stay, Summer," Clay urged. "There's always room for two more."

"I didn't invite you, either," she returned without hesitation.

"Three more, then," he amended with his best toothpaste-ad smile. "You wouldn't deny us the opportunity to get to know your beautiful sister, would you?"

Deny him, deny him, Spring silently begged.

Summer looked straight into her sister's eyes, quite obviously read her thoughts and laughed. "Okay, you can stay," she told Clay, winking impudently at Spring. "It'll give Spring something to write in her diary."

Clay slipped an arm around Spring's stiff shoulders. "I'm very good at providing diary material," he murmured into her ear.

"I'm sure you are," Spring replied, adroitly sidestepping his loose embrace. "But I prefer to fill my diary with *non*fiction."

With one of his rare grins creasing his lean cheeks Derek punched Clay lightly on the shoulder. "You may have just met your match, my man."

Clay smiled at Spring in a way that melted her lower vertebrae. "You know, Derek, you just might be right," he answered.

"OH, SPRING, it's so good to see you." Summer hugged her sister hard, then returned to the lettuce she was shredding for a salad. "It seems like so long since we've been together."

Neatly slicing a plump tomato, Spring smiled somewhat sadly, thinking of how little time she was able to spend with her sisters now that they were all grown and could really enjoy being together. "It has been a long time. I've missed you."

"Me, too. Of course, the telephone company loves me."

Spring laughed. "We should both own stock by now. Every month I pay for calls to you in California, to Autumn in Florida and to Mom and Dad in Rose Bud. The phone bill's almost as high as my rent."

"Derek's never complained about ours, but he always takes a deep breath before he opens the envelope."

"I like him, Summer."

Summer glowed. "I'm glad. I knew you would. The two of you have a lot in common, actually. I told him that the day after I met him."

"Did you?" Spring cut the last tomato and reached for a cucumber. "I loved the letters you sent me about your, um, unusual courtship. Swept you right off your feet, didn't he?"

"I'll say," Summer agreed with a laugh. "He told me he loved me exactly one week and two days after we met. Scared me witless."

"Why?"

"I thought it was infatuation, that he'd change his mind after getting to know me better. I was already so crazy about him by then that I knew I'd be destroyed if he left. Thank God he was able to convince me that what he felt was real."

Spring sighed wistfully. "I envy you, Summer. You and Derek look so happy. So do Connie and Joel."

Summer turned and leaned back against the counter, studying her sister's face. "So what happened between you and Roger? All I know is that you were seeing him steadily for several months and then you stopped."

Spring tried to look as if she were concentrating on the cucumber in front of her. "Nothing really happened," she replied vaguely. "It just didn't work out."

"Funny, that's exactly the same thing you said when you broke up with James and then Gary."

"So what can I say?" Spring asked lightly. "None of them worked out. I guess I'm just not cut out for permanence in my relationships."

"Don't give me that. You wouldn't envy Connie and me so much if you didn't want the same thing for yourself. I've always thought you were the type who wanted marriage and children as well as your career."

"I do," Spring confessed. "Very much. But every time I start thinking of permanence with any of the men I've dated, I begin to back out of the relationship. I must be more attached to my single state than I realize."

"Or maybe you prefer your single state over marriage to any of the men you've dated," Summer countered. "I never met Roger, but if he was anything like James and Gary, we're talking b-o-r-i-n-g."

"They weren't—Well, maybe they were a little boring, but they were all fine, respectable men."

"So maybe you don't want a fine, respectable man. Maybe what you need is a bit of a scoundrel."

"Don't be ridiculous."

"Who's being ridiculous?" Summer demanded. "This is your sister you're talking to, Spring Deborah Reed. I know who your heroes were when you were growing up. You drooled over old Clark Gable films, you kept a poster of Burt Reynolds taped to your closet door and *M*A*S*H* was your all-time favorite television program because Hawkeye Pierce made you break out in a sweat. More recently you've had a not-so-secret crush on Harrison Ford. These are not fine, respectable men, Sis. They're scoundrels."

"All very well for fantasy, but not for real life. Look at me, Summer. I'm an average, unexciting optometrist who is perfectly content to live her entire life in Little Rock, Arkansas. I'm not exactly Carole Lombard, who wouldn't have been happy with anything but a scoundrel, as you put it."

"I *am* looking at you," Summer replied seriously. "I see a beautiful blonde who's always had to be the responsible big sister, the pride and joy of the Reed family, the only one in several generations to finish college and go on to graduate work. The only one ever to earn the title Doctor."

"A term of respect. I'm not an M.D."

"But you're a damned good optometrist. You've told me so many times," Summer added with a smile. "You're also bored. Admit it."

Spring abandoned the cucumber. "Okay," she conceded, turning to face her sister. "Sometimes I get a little bored. Not with my work—I love that. But my personal life is not exactly scintillating. If I kept a diary, it would look very little different than my appointment calendar at the office. Not just nonfiction but noninteresting."

"So what are you going to do about it?"

"I have no idea. What would you suggest?"

"Fall madly in love, get married and have a houseful of kids," Summer suggested promptly.

"Sounds lovely, but since I'm not even dating anyone at this time, it's a bit impractical."

"Okay, so have an affair. A crazy, no-strings-attached, passionate affair. Clay's already volunteered, as a matter of fact."

Spring flushed vividly. "You discussed this with that . . . with Clay?"

"Only a little," Summer answered with mock innocence. "He thought my idea was brilliant."

"Someday, Summer Linda Reed, I am going to kill you. Slowly," Spring added, pushing irritably at her glasses, which were beginning to slide down her nose. "Besides, if I *were* going to have an affair—which I'm not—it certainly wouldn't be with Clay."

"What's wrong with Clay?"

"My God, Summer, how can you even ask? The way he's dressed, the way he acts—definitely not my type."

"Do you always judge people by appearances, Spring? When are you going to learn that a three-piece suit and a tie don't make a man? Clay's a wonderful, caring person. He loves to laugh and tease—as he did with you—and he's warm and very demonstrative in his affections. He's always got his arm around someone. As a matter of fact, Derek threatened to break that arm a few times before he realized that Clay wasn't getting too cozy with me. It's a shame there aren't more men who are as comfortable with their feelings and emotions as Clay. Yes, he dresses a bit oddly, but even that is due to his lively sense of humor. He likes making people smile."

It wasn't the first time that Spring had been chastised by her younger sister for her conservative nature—or made to feel vaguely guilty about those circumspect tendencies. "He's just not my type," she reiterated somewhat gruffly. "That man is strange, Summer."

"True," Summer agreed gravely. "But he's certainly not boring."

No, Spring didn't think Clay McEntire would ever be called boring. A lot of other things, maybe, but never boring.

"There's the doorbell," Summer said unnecessarily, sparing Spring the need to comment further on Clay

McEntire. "Our pizzas are here. Connie should have the table set by now, so would you give me a hand with the salad stuff?"

"Sure." Spring turned and gathered an armful of forks and salad bowls, then found herself taking a deep breath for courage before joining the others in the dining room. She had to ask herself why she felt that she needed courage. She didn't have to answer herself, though, because the first person she saw when she entered the room was Clay. And he looked even better now than he had before, if that was possible. Damn.

2

THE DINNER WAS certainly...interesting, Spring thought some time later. She hadn't heard such snappy repartee since the last Neil Simon movie she'd seen. Summer, of course, was a compulsive cutup, and Connie was just like her. With their dry wit and subtle humor Derek and Joel made perfect counterpoints to their irrepressible mates. And Clay...

Clay. Spring wasn't sure exactly how she felt about Clay. She was definitely attracted to him; there was no question about that. And she thought that perhaps he was as attracted to her. He was funny, he was charming, he was exciting. Maybe Summer was right about Spring having a weakness for scoundrels. Of course, she also dearly loved strawberry shortcake, but she knew better than to indulge. She was allergic to strawberries.

The frivolity continued after dinner, when everyone moved to the den for a game of Trivial Pursuit. Spring found herself partnered with Clay, which gave him an excuse to sit close beside her on a cozy love seat. She tried very hard to pay attention to the game, but how could she concentrate on History or Art and Literature when there was such a gorgeous male draping himself all over her? She was, after all, only human.

When she found herself mentally counting the number of times his enticingly close chest rose and fell with his breathing, she knew she needed a few moments alone to get control of herself. Summer called an intermission so that she could make coffee and slice a chocolate cake, and Spring took advantage of the opportunity to slip down the hallway to the guest room, where Derek had carried her bags.

There she plopped down on the edge of the bed, not even noticing the lovely decor of the tastefully frilly room as she wondered what on earth was wrong with her. It was almost as if in leaving Little Rock she'd left behind the rigid code of responsible behavior that she'd lived by for as long as she could remember. She wasn't normally attracted to offbeat, probably shallow men such as Clay McEntire. In Little Rock she wouldn't have looked twice at such a man. Well, she amended, she might have looked. More than twice. But would she have found him so utterly fascinating?

She found herself wondering if he really had volunteered to have a passionate affair with her. Would he be as unpredictable in bed as he was out of it? She suspected that he would be imaginative, sensitive, considerate, and just downright good.

"Oh, my God, what am I doing?" she groaned, shaking her head to dispel any such thoughts. "I just met the man, for pete's sake." She had never indulged in casual, recreational sex, nor was she about to begin now. "I'm not," she repeated out loud for emphasis.

She stood and glared determinedly into the mirror on one wall of the bedroom. She looked the same as usual. Hair still properly pinned on top of her head, white silk blouse neatly tucked into the waistband of the straight heather-pink skirt that matched the jacket she'd discarded earlier. She hadn't changed at all since arriving in California. Nor would she.

"Right," she said, nodding crisply at her reflection. Then she stepped out of the door of her bedroom and straight into the arms of Clay McEntire.

"Sorry," he murmured, though he didn't look at all sorry to find himself standing in the hallway with his arms around her. "Are you okay?"

"I'm fine," she replied. Dammit, her voice had gone all breathless again, she noticed in disgust. "What are you doing?" Was he following her?

His lovely blue-green eyes twinkled with mischievous amusement as he nodded toward the door beside her bedroom. "That's the bathroom," he replied. "I had planned on visiting it. Okay with you?"

She flushed, trying to disengage herself from the strong arms that had tightened around her slim waist. "You certainly don't need my permission."

"For anything?"

"Of course not," she answered curtly, squirming against him. The movement made her want to groan with the pleasure-pain it caused her.

"Oh, in that case—" He smothered his own words against her mouth as he leaned her back against the wall and kissed her with painstaking thoroughness.

Had it been possible, Spring would have gulped. As it was, she went rigid with surprise. Much later she would try to convince herself that she'd parted her lips only to protest his impertinence. But whatever the reason, her action gave him the perfect opportunity to deepen the kiss—and he did.

Her fists clenched his shoulders when his tongue swept the inside of her mouth, exploring and claiming it. At the same time his hands began an exploration of their own, sweeping from her shoulders to her hips in long, arousing strokes. Spring moaned low in her chest, her eyes closing behind the glasses that were pressed crookedly between their faces. When she found herself wishing the glasses were out of the way so that the kiss could continue more comfortably, she opened her eyes wide and renewed her struggle to free herself. She twisted her head so that the kiss was broken and shoved against him with all her strength. "What are you doing?"

He chuckled shakily, though he allowed her to put several inches between them. "This time I think the answer is obvious, sweet Spring. I'm trying to seduce you."

"You—" She stopped to swallow. "Oh."

He laughed. "Yes, oh. You're enchanting, did you know that? May I kiss you again, or do you still insist that I don't need your permission?"

"No! I mean, no, you can't kiss me again. Clay, I don't even know you!"

"*That* situation can easily be changed," he murmured meaningfully, lifting a hand to trace her slightly swollen lower lip.

"No." She shook her head emphatically. "I'm only going to be here for twelve days, Clay."

"That's plenty of time," he replied, unperturbed, his fingers stroking her cheek.

"Look, I know things are . . . different in California, but I'm from Arkansas and I don't, well, to be blunt, I don't sleep with just anyone I happen to find attractive. So whatever Summer may have told you, I'm not interested in a vacation affair."

"Okay, so seduction is out," Clay replied cheerfully. A little too cheerfully, Spring thought with illogical resentment. Couldn't he at least have made a token protest? "How about friendship?" he continued. "Are you interested in making a new friend on your vacation, sweet Spring?"

"It *is* possible that we could be friends," Spring agreed cautiously. "But only on one condition."

"What's that?" he inquired, his fingers moving to the vulnerable spot just behind her ear.

"Stop calling me 'sweet Spring.'"

Clay laughed. "Fair enough." He kissed her cheek, briefly, barely touching her, then moved away. "If you'll excuse me, I think I'll visit that room next door."

He paused at the doorway of the bathroom. "Oh, and, Spring?"

"Yes?"

"I don't sleep with just anyone, either. I don't happen to think Arkansans and Californians are all that different." He shut the door behind him as he entered the bathroom, leaving her standing in the hallway with her mouth open.

Moments later Spring stood once again before the mirror in her bedroom. Only this time the woman who stared back at her looked slightly different. Her neat knot of hair had loosened, allowing more tendrils to fall around her flushed face, her glasses were crooked and the white silk blouse was only halfway tucked into her skirt. Her sister had been right about one thing, she thought as she tried to straighten her appearance. Clay certainly was a toucher!

Summer had been right about something else, she added to herself in wary bemusement.

Clay certainly was *not* boring.

A short time later Spring toyed with the slice of cake her sister had served her, studiously avoiding Clay's gaze, though she could feel him watching her with laughter dancing in his eyes. Whether he was enjoying a private joke with her or simply laughing at her provincial response to his blatant pass, she didn't know. Nor did she attempt to guess. She was much too busy trying to forget the feel of his lips on hers and his arms around her.

The extension telephone hidden discreetly in a carved wooden box on a glossy end table rang, and Summer, who was closest, answered it. The others in the room lowered their conversation for her benefit, so everyone heard her say, "Frank? What's wrong?"

She listened for a moment, then exclaimed, "Oh, no! When?"

Clay straightened abruptly on the love seat beside Spring, his full attention directed to Summer. Spring noticed that her sister's eyes turned immediately in Clay's direction as she listened to the person on the other end of the line. "Yes, he's here," Summer said into the receiver. "I'll tell him. Please call me if you hear anything, Frank."

Before she'd even replaced the receiver in the box, Clay was up, standing over Summer's chair as he demanded, "What's wrong? What did Frank want?"

"Thelma Sawyer has run away again," Summer answered with a deep sigh. "She hasn't been home in a week. Her mother just got around to contacting Frank to ask if he's seen her."

Clay flinched visibly and shoved his hand through his thick golden hair. "Damn. What happened?"

"Frank said she had another fight with her mother." Summer pushed herself out of her chair and looked up at Clay. "What will happen to her this time, Clay? Will they let her go back to Halloran?"

"Not likely," Clay answered briefly.

Spring watched them closely, thinking that Clay looked somehow older than he had only a few minutes earlier. She knew that her sister worked part-time at Halloran House, a home for troubled teenagers, while she attended classes to obtain a degree in education so that she could work with the young people full-time. Spring hadn't known that Clay was in any way involved with the project.

"Clay," Summer said softly, leaning into Derek's arm as he offered comfort to his obviously distressed wife. "What if she gets into trouble again?"

Clay exhaled. "I don't know, Summer," he admitted. He straightened abruptly. "I'm going out to look for her."

"I'll go with you."

"No." He shook his head at Summer's offer. "You stay here with your guests. I'm going to check with some of Thelma's friends and a few other sources. I'll call you if I find out anything."

"You'd better." Summer tugged him downward so that she could kiss his cheek. "Good luck."

"Yeah." Clay bade good-night to the others, then turned to Spring. "I'll see you again, sweet, uh, Spring," he corrected himself with a weak facsimile of his devilish smile.

"Good night, Clay," Spring answered, surreptitiously eyeing the lines that had suddenly appeared around his eyes. Perhaps he wasn't as shallow as she'd first thought, she decided, watching him leave. The news of Thelma's disappearance had obviously shaken him badly.

"This is really a shame," Connie said as Spring turned her attention back to the others. "Thelma can be so sweet. That mother of hers ought to be locked up for treating her daughter so badly."

"Oh, they can't do that," Summer answered bitterly. "Mrs. Sawyer doesn't physically abuse Thelma. The state chooses to ignore verbal abuse. After all, that kind doesn't leave bruises—none that show, anyway."

"This is rough on poor Clay." Connie twisted a copper-red curl around one scarlet-tipped finger, her expression sympathetic. "Thelma's always been one of his favorites, hasn't she?"

"Yes."

"Yours, too," Derek murmured to Summer, his arm tightening around her shoulders. "I'm sorry, darling. Is there anything I can do to help?"

Summer shook her head. "If anyone can find her, Clay can. I just hope he's not too late."

"How old is Thelma?" Spring asked.

"Fifteen," Summer whispered miserably. "She's only fifteen, dammit."

Spring bit her lower lip. "That's so young. I wonder where she'll go?"

Summer shrugged. "Who knows? The streets are full of runaways. They develop a talent for not being seen. She may even have left town, though she never has before. It's not the first time she's run away," she explained, "but last time she got into so much trouble that Clay almost couldn't bail her out. He was able to get her readmitted as a resident at Halloran House then, but I don't think he'll be able to now. Halloran House is only for those kids who aren't considered to be truly hard cases. Most of them are there at the insistence of their parents rather than the juvenile courts."

"What does Clay have to do with Halloran House?" Spring finally asked, unable to contain her curiosity any longer.

"Haven't I mentioned that?" Summer asked, surprised. "Clay was one of the people responsible for getting Halloran House started a few years ago. He's on the board of directors and he spends most of his spare time there, counseling the kids."

"Counseling?"

"Yes. He has a Ph.D. in adolescent psychology. He could be making a fortune in private practice, but instead, he's a counselor for a public junior-high school in San Francisco."

Spring had risen when Clay left. Now she abruptly sat back down. Clay McEntire had a doctorate in psychology? So much for appearances, she told herself wryly.

The call from Frank—whom Spring discovered to be Frank Rivers, the live-in director of Halloran House—had cast a pall over the evening, so Connie and Joel left not long after Clay departed.

"You must be tired, Spring. Would you like to turn in now?" Summer asked shortly afterward. It was past ten o'clock—past midnight, Arkansas time—and Spring *was* tired.

The two sisters chatted contentedly while Spring pulled on a lacy blue gown and brushed out her shoulder-length, silvery blond hair. They mentioned their parents back home in Rose Bud, Arkansas, and chuckled together over their fiery-tempered, ultraliberated sister Autumn. Twenty-four-year-old Autumn lived in Tampa, Florida, where she worked as an electrician, and her sisters always enjoyed swapping stories about her.

After a few minutes of pleasant conversation, Summer asked with suspicious nonchalance, "Is Connie anything like you'd pictured her?"

"She's exactly like I imagined she would be," Spring replied with a smile. "I like her."

"And Joel? Did you like him, too?"

"Yes, very much." Spring swallowed, knowing what was coming next. She was right.

"So," Summer went on casually, "what did you think of Clay, once you got past your first impression of him?"

Spring looked quickly down at the blouse she was folding, allowing her shoulder-length hair to hide her suddenly rosy face. Just the mention of Clay's name had taken her back to that interlude in the hallway. She could almost feel him next to her once more, and the sensation made her pulse react again with a crazy rhythm. "He was very, um . . ." Her voice trailed off for lack of words.

"Very 'um'?" Summer demanded quizzically. "What's 'um'? Sexy? Good-looking? Intriguing? Irresistible?"

"Okay, so he's about the most gorgeous thing I've ever seen off a movie screen," Spring admitted abruptly, glaring at her sister's smug grin. "But I still think he's strange."

"I tried to fix him up with Autumn. I thought they'd make a terrific couple. They got along great when she was here for my wedding, but unfortunately, there was just no chemistry. He never even made a pass at her," Summer complained.

"Clay and Autumn?" Spring repeated distastefully, hating the suggestion but refusing to acknowledge why. "What a dumb idea."

"Oh, you think so?" Summer asked innocently.

"Yes, I do."

"Well, then, how about Clay and Spring?"

"An even dumber idea," Spring muttered, her flush deepening.

"You know, I would have said the same thing yesterday. Now, well, maybe it's not such a dumb idea, after all," Summer mused with a grin.

"Good night, Summer," Spring said pointedly, nodding toward the door.

Summer laughed, then sobered. "I'm glad you're here, Spring," she said again. "I know we haven't had much in common in the past, but I love you, Sis. Besides, it's so nice to hear an Arkansas accent again—other than mine."

Spring chuckled, her mild irritation evaporating immediately. "I love you, too, Summer. I'm really looking forward to spending this time with you and Derek."

"It just might be interesting," Summer commented, then ducked out the door before Spring could ask what she'd meant.

CLAY GROANED, rolled over and promptly fell onto the floor. Cursing under his breath, he sat up, combing his hair out of his eyes with his fingers, and tried to orient himself. He'd searched for Thelma most of the night, coming home around dawn so exhausted that he hadn't even made it to the bedroom. He'd fallen asleep on the couch, still fully dressed except for his shoes. Pushing himself painfully to his feet, he noted that he looked like an unmade bed and smelled like a horse. A glance at his watch told him that it was close to ll:00 a.m. Tugging off his wrinkled shirt, he headed for the shower.

Half an hour later he felt somewhat more human. He dressed in loose, double-pleated black slacks, a black-

and-white cotton shirt in a bold geometric print and a crisp winter-white blazer, pushing the sleeves up on his forearms as he dug in the closet for shoes. The ones he selected were canvas deck shoes, the uppers printed in a black-and-white checkerboard pattern. He never considered wearing socks.

He went through the motions of dressing mechanically, hardly conscious of making decisions on what to wear. He was thinking about Spring. He had thought about Spring since the moment his abrupt contact with his living-room floor had awakened him. He hadn't stopped thinking about Spring since he'd looked up the night before and seen her standing in the doorway to Summer's den. Even when he'd walked the sleaziest back streets of San Francisco during the wee hours of the morning, doggedly searching for one frightened, defiant young black girl, he hadn't been able to rid his mind entirely of the beautiful blonde he'd kissed earlier.

His first impression of her—that she'd been a snob— just might have been wrong. By the end of the evening he'd found himself liking her. A lot. Oh, she was different from Summer; he'd grant that. Quieter, more inhibited, perhaps even a bit shy. Different, too, from the women he usually dated, but in a nice way.

There hadn't been many women in his life lately, other than friends. In fact, there hadn't been *any* special woman in his life since he'd stopped seeing Jessica Dixon some four months earlier. Jessica had been amusing, outrageous and beautiful, and he'd enjoyed being with her until she'd finally gotten tired of her undeniably second-place status in his life and had broken off with him in a rather ugly scene when he'd been called away from a party to bail one of his kids out of jail. He'd never made any pretense that their relationship was anything more than casual, nor had he apologized to her for the long hours he'd spent with the students and other young people he counseled. There had been times when he hadn't called her or seen her for days—sometimes for as long as a couple of weeks. He hadn't realized that she'd wanted more. He was rather ashamed to acknowledge that he hadn't really missed her.

But it couldn't be just an overlong period of celibacy that drew him so strongly to Spring Reed. After all, there had been other women during the past four months he'd found attractive, but he hadn't wanted any of them enough to do anything about it. And certainly none of them had interfered with his concentration while he was dealing with a crisis with one of his kids.

What was it about her that did this to him? It wasn't just her looks; he'd established that. Not just a need for a woman. So what? The slightly shy, intelligent glimmer in beguilingly uptilted eyes? The low gurgle of laughter that had escaped her so often during that lighthearted pizza dinner? The musical cadence of her Southern-accented voice? The way her rounded chin had firmed and lifted when she'd informed him that she didn't sleep around? Or maybe the way she'd responded so heatedly when he'd kissed her.

He wanted to see her again, find out more about the woman who'd intrigued him so. But right now he was going to continue his search for Thelma.

"OH, MY GOD, you've been mall hopping." Derek's voice was resigned as he took in the sizable stack of packages piled on the floor of his den.

The two sisters, both exhausted, looked up guiltily from their slumped positions in matching easy chairs. "We shopped a little," Summer admitted.

"A little?" Derek looked again at the tall, colorful mountain of packages. "I thought you were going sight-seeing."

"We did," Spring said with a tired smile. "We saw every shopping sight in San Francisco and Sausalito."

"I suppose you both have smoking plastic cards in your purses?"

"Guilty as charged, your honor," Summer quipped. "We went nuts. But I did buy you a new tie, if it makes you feel any better."

"How very generous of you," Derek murmured, passing the knee-high heap of purchases on his way to the bar.

"Yes, I thought so," Summer answered complacently. She shoved herself reluctantly out of the chair. "I suppose I really should shower before changing for dinner. You did say you were taking us out tonight, didn't you, darling?"

"Yes, I think I did say that," Derek replied, splashing ice-cold orange juice into a glass. "Choose someplace cheap, will you? There are still ten full shopping days left of your sister's vacation."

Spring smiled, watching as Summer kissed her husband lovingly. It was quite obvious that Summer could buy out all of Marin County and Derek wouldn't care in the least. It was also perfectly evident that Summer would never do anything that would truly upset Derek. Not for the first time, Spring had to fight down a surge of envy at her sister's good fortune.

"How was your racquetball game?" Summer asked her husband, watching as he thirstily downed the orange juice and reached for a refill.

"Strenuous," Derek answered with a grimace. "But I managed to make a decent showing."

Summer laughed. "Not bad, considering your propensity to pit yourself against twenty-five-year-old jocks." She kissed him again before she left the room, her limp more pronounced than usual, testimony to the strenuous shopping spree.

"She's tired," Derek commented, taking a seat close to Spring and stretching out to rest as he finished his juice.

She, too, had watched Summer limp away. "Yes, I know. I was just feeling guilty."

"Don't. It would take a bigger person than you to stop her once she decides she wants to go shopping. And she's delighted to have you here. She misses seeing her family."

Hardly aware of speaking aloud, Spring murmured, "She's changed."

"In what way?"

Spring absently pushed her glasses up on her nose and shrugged slightly. "I don't know, exactly. Grown up, I guess. I still can't help looking at her from a big sister's viewpoint."

"How do you like the way she's turned out?"

"I like it very much," Spring replied decisively. "She's happy, she has a direction to her life now that she's returned to school and she's learned to share her feelings more."

"And yet she still knows how to play," Derek added. "That's a special part of her. One that I needed very much."

Spring cocked her head back against her chair and eyed her brother-in-law. "Summer thinks you and I are a lot alike."

Derek nodded. "Yes, I know. I suppose she's right, in some ways. We're both organized and ambitious and rather serious, on the whole."

"Not necessarily admirable qualities from Summer's point of view."

"Ah, but she loves us both," Derek reminded her.

"True. You're exactly what she needed in a husband. She probably thinks I need someone exactly like *her*."

"Someone like Clay McEntire?" Derek murmured with a half smile. When Spring's eyes narrowed, he explained, "She seemed to find the idea rather intriguing after you went to bed last night."

"It's ridiculous, of course."

"Of course." Derek's voice was just a bit too innocuous.

Spring shot him a suspicious look. "You wouldn't happen to agree with her, would you, Derek?"

"I make it a practice never to play matchmaker," Derek informed her solemnly, "despite what Summer and Connie refer to as my compulsive habit of offering advice. A hazard of being a business consultant, I suppose."

"Whatever, I have absolutely no interest in Clay McEntire," Spring stated categorically, even as she wondered whether she was trying to convince Derek or herself.

"I'm very sorry to hear that," said an already familiar voice from behind her. "Clay McEntire is most definitely interested in you."

3

SPRING STARTED and jerked her head toward the doorway, finding the very person she'd just named lounging there with a look of amusement on his much-too-handsome face. She realized that her sister must have let him in. She could think of absolutely nothing to say.

Taking pity on her, Derek spoke. "What's up, Clay? Heard anything about Thelma?"

"Not a thing," Clay answered, suddenly grim. "If anyone knows where she is, they're not talking."

Spring lifted her eyes from his unusual black-and-white ensemble to note that he looked tired. Tired and rather despondent. She was startled to find herself wanting to cheer him up. She missed his easy smile. "Can't you file a missing-persons report on her?" she asked curiously.

"Her mother did that last week. Thelma's run away before, though, and there are so many other missing-persons reports filed each week that the cops tend to give them low priority unless they have a real lead. I'm not too crazy about having the cops haul a kid back home, anyway, unless there is no other alternative."

"Can I get you something to drink, Clay?" Derek asked.

"No, thanks, Derek. I just wanted to tell Summer that I haven't been able to find Thelma."

Derek lifted one eyebrow but refrained from pointing out that Clay hadn't needed to drive into Sausalito when a telephone call would have sufficed. Spring frowned, well aware of that herself.

"In that case," Derek asked, "would you like to join us for dinner? We're going out."

Sprawled in the easy chair Summer had abandoned, Clay nudged the pile of packages on the floor before him with one black-and-white-clad foot. "Sure you can afford that? Or were all these purchases made with Arkansas money?" he teased, smiling at Spring.

"I bought my share," Spring admitted with a shy attempt at friendliness. She was very much aware that Clay had not yet accepted or declined Derek's invitation to join them for dinner. She wasn't sure which option she preferred him to take. Suddenly and inexplicably nervous, she stood and began to gather the much-discussed packages. "I suppose I should start freshening up for dinner."

"Let me help you with those," Clay volunteered immediately, jumping to his feet.

"Oh, that's not—"

But he'd already grabbed an armload and was headed for the hallway that led to the guest room. Spring pointedly avoided Derek's amused gaze as she followed Clay.

"Where do you want these?"

"Just throw them on the bed," she replied, walking past him to do so with hers.

He grinned tantalizingly and muttered something that she thought sounded vaguely like, "I'd like to throw *you* on the bed," but prudence kept her from asking him to repeat himself.

Instead, she waited until he'd unloaded his arms, then commented, "You look tired. Have you been searching for Thelma all day?"

"And most of last night," he admitted, running his fingers through his luxurious hair, his grin fading.

"Didn't you get any sleep at all?"

"About five hours. Why? Are you concerned?" he asked with interest.

She shrugged, toying with a button on her lavender cotton shirt to avoid looking at him.

When it was obvious that Spring wasn't going to answer his question, Clay shoved his hands into the deep pockets of his slightly wrinkled black slacks and flicked a glance around the room. "Are you enjoying your visit with your sister?"

"Yes."

"Did you have a good time on your shopping spree?"

"Yes."

"Do you want to have an affair with me?"

Spring almost choked. "No," she managed at last, hoping she looked more sincere than she felt.

"Do you like going to plays?"

The man was certifiable. Deciding that the course of least resistance was to humor him, Spring nodded slowly. "Yes."

"I have tickets for an opening Monday night. Will you go with me?"

"I, uh—"

"I'm only inviting you to a play, Spring, not an orgy," he told her with mock impatience. Then he added with a near smirk, "Although I'd be happy to arrange the latter, if you like."

"I think we'd better stick with the play," Spring answered hastily.

He grinned. "Okay, I'll pick you up at six-thirty. It starts early."

She'd just agreed to a date with him, Spring realized belatedly. She started to tell him she'd changed her mind, then stopped as she focused again on those tiny, weary lines at the corners of his eyes. Damn her soft-heartedness, she thought with a resigned sigh. She wouldn't change her mind. "Fine. Now if you'll excuse me, I need to freshen up for dinner."

"Okay." He dropped a kiss on her lips as he passed her. "See you Monday."

Her entire body tingling from that too-brief contact, Spring spoke before he was completely out of the room, detaining him. "Aren't you joining us for dinner?"

He looked back at her. "Not tonight. I'm going back out on the streets."

"But—" She stopped, then shrugged slightly and continued, "You look so tired. And you have to eat."

His handsome face softened and his mouth dipped into a warm smile, as if her concern pleased him. "I'll grab a sandwich. And I'll try to get more sleep tonight. But I have to find Thelma, if I can."

She nodded, aware of her acute disappointment and annoyed with herself for feeling it. "Good luck."

"Thank you, Spring." He looked at her for a moment longer, then left, closing her door behind him.

Spring stood so long staring at that closed door that she was almost late for dinner.

DEREK'S SECRETARY, who'd been on maternity leave for the past month, had her baby Saturday night. Summer and Derek felt obligated to pay a brief visit to the hospital on Sunday. They invited Spring to join them, but she begged off. She had always been a person who needed time alone occasionally, and knowing that,

Summer did not press her to go. Promising to be back soon, Summer and Derek left shortly after lunch.

Spring relished the time to herself. As much as she was enjoying her visit, it felt good to kick off her shoes, stretch out on a lounge chair by the pool on this unseasonably warm March afternoon and dive into the pages of a book she'd brought with her from home. She had dressed more casually than was her habit in a long-sleeved aqua-and-white-print cotton pullover and snug, matching aqua jeans. Her hair was in its usual soft knot on top of her head, and she wore a minimum of makeup. She was comfortable, contented and relaxed.

Until a rich male voice interrupted her solitude and shattered her peaceful idyll. "Now this is a lovely picture."

Spring jumped, dropping her book, and jerked her head around. "Clay!" she exclaimed, her pulse racing—because he'd surprised her or because he looked so incredibly sexy? She didn't choose to analyze. He wore jeans, washed-soft Levi's worn almost white at the knees and seat and button fly. Red tennis shoes matched his old-fashioned red suspenders. The sleeves of a blue chambray work shirt were turned up on his forearms, and a battered tweed cap completed his outfit. "You startled me," she accused him breathlessly.

"I'm sorry," he apologized. "I didn't mean to. I thought I saw someone back here when I drove up, and when no one answered the doorbell, I decided to come around and see."

She eyed his clothing. "You look like the president of the Roy Underhill fan club," she told him.

Clay's blond eyebrows shot up in surprise. "Now how do you know who Roy Underhill is? Are you into woodworking?"

"Not really. But I am into remodeling old homes—theoretically, anyway—and Roy Underhill's *The Woodwright Shop* comes on PBS just before Bob Vila's *This Old House* on Sunday afternoons at home. So are you an Underhill fan?"

"As a matter of fact, I have both of his books at home in my workshop," Clay confessed. "I love working with wood."

"Are you any good?" she asked curiously.

"Oh, I'm good," he replied audaciously. "I'd be happy to demonstrate at any time."

She just managed not to blush at his innuendo by busying herself with swinging her legs over the side of her chair and sliding her feet into her white flats. "I'll let you know if I'm interested," she informed him coolly, her tone implying that the time would never come.

"You do that," he answered, his eyes telling her that it would—and sooner than she expected. "Summer's not home?"

"No, she and Derek went to the hospital to see his secretary's new baby. They should be back in another hour or so."

"What did she have? Boy or girl?" Clay inquired as he draped himself into the chair beside Spring's.

"Boy."

"That's nice."

Since he seemed to be settled in, Spring decided she might as well play hostess. "Can I get you something to drink, Clay?"

"No, thanks. Maybe later." He smiled at her, apparently quite content to be with her on this pleasant afternoon.

She relaxed a bit, silently admitting that she was content with his company, as well. If only she weren't so aware of how very attractive he looked in the afternoon sun, how well the soft fabric of his shirt and worn jeans defined his lean muscles. "Have you heard anything more about Thelma?" she asked to distract herself.

He shook his head. "No. I've got a lot of feelers out, but no leads so far. I'm pretty sure she's still in the area, but she's well hidden."

"I hope she's all right."

"So do I. What are you reading?" he inquired, deliberately changing the solemn subject.

"It's a new one by—" She stopped when the cordless telephone that she'd carried out with her earlier rang. Derek was expecting a business call later, and he'd asked her to take a message if it came in while he was away. She reached out to answer the phone, picking up the pencil and pad beside it. A moment later she held out the receiver to Clay. "It's for you. It's Frank."

"Thanks. Hi, Frank, what's up? *What?* When? Where is she? Yeah, I know where that is. Okay, I'm on my way. I'll call you later. Thanks."

He was on his feet immediately, dropping the phone onto the glass-topped patio table. "Frank's got a lead on Thelma. One of her friends broke down and told him where she's been staying. He thinks she may be ill. Tell Summer I'll call her later, will you?"

"Clay," Spring said suddenly, when he appeared to be on the verge of leaving. "Would you . . . ?" She faltered when he turned to look questioningly at her.

"What is it, Spring?"

"I could go with you, if you'd like," she offered in a rush of words. When he looked surprised, she hurried to add, "I just thought I could help. If you think I'd only be in the way, I'll understand."

He smiled at her, that deep-cornered, male-model smile that made her leg bones soften. "Why, thank you, Spring. I would like for you to go with me."

"You're sure?"

"If you are. We won't be going into the nicer part of town."

She nodded, gathering her things and the cordless telephone to carry them into the house. "I didn't think we would be. Just let me leave a note for Summer."

"I'll wait for you in the car."

Even as she scribbled the note for her sister, Spring asked herself why she'd volunteered to accompany Clay. He obviously didn't need her help. Spring grudgingly suspected that the reason she'd suddenly offered to join Clay had been that she hadn't wanted to see him walk away. She had *definitely* left her common sense back home in Little Rock, she concluded, even as she grabbed her purse and locked all the doors.

Spring wasn't particularly surprised to discover that Clay's car was a fire-engine-red Mazda RX-7. It was exactly the type of car that she would have expected him to drive. Of course, she would have been no more surprised to find him in a psychedelic-painted van, circa 1968 San Francisco. Come to think of it, she mused, there wasn't much Clay McEntire could do that *would* surprise her.

"How old are you, Clay?" she asked as the powerful sports car sped them across the Golden Gate Bridge.

He shot her a sideways glance before answering the first question she'd asked since they'd left her sister's house. "I'll be thirty-five in June. How old do you think I look?"

She thought about that one for a moment before answering honestly. "Anywhere from mid-twenties to late-thirties, depending on your expression."

He grinned. "Guess I'll have to practice that mid-twenties expression."

She didn't bother to tell him that he looked equally devastating either way. She figured he already knew it. There had to be mirrors in his home. She wondered where he lived. And then she wondered with whom. Shifting in her seat, she searched her mind for an innocuous topic of conversation, something that would keep him from worrying about Thelma until they reached their destination, finally settling on his work. "Summer tells me that you have a Ph.D. in adolescent psychology."

"Yes."

"Do you enjoy counseling in public schools?"

"I wouldn't be doing it if I didn't enjoy it."

"No," she murmured. "You wouldn't, would you?" She couldn't imagine Clay doing anything he didn't enjoy. Unlike herself, who often acted from her overdeveloped sense of duty and responsibility at the price of personal pleasure. People like Clay, and like Summer, had a way of taking whatever life handed them and making it suit their own purposes. Spring wished she knew their secret.

"What about you?" Clay asked suddenly.

"What about me?"

"Do you ever get bored passing out prescriptions for reading glasses?"

"I might, if that was all I did. It's not. Only recently I had a patient—eight years old—who's been classified as mentally handicapped. His teacher recommended that the boy be placed in special classes for children with learning disabilities, despite his parents' belief that their son had an average IQ. After trying tutors and child psychologists they brought him to me. We discovered that he had a visual impairment—an inability to process the two separate images detected by his eyes, to put it simply. He's really a very bright child, considering what he's had to deal with. My job is particularly rewarding when children are involved."

"That sounds fascinating," Clay conceded, and the look he turned to her was sincere. "And it seems that we have something in common if you enjoy dealing with childhood problems."

She lowered her chin and toyed modestly with her seat belt. "Not all my cases are like that," she admitted. "Most of the time I *do* pass out prescriptions for reading glasses. But I love my work."

He reached across the console to catch her left hand in his right one. "I wasn't trying to offend you when I asked that question. Sometimes I don't mean things exactly the way they leave my mouth."

"I understand. And there was no offense taken," she assured him.

"You're a very special person, Spring Reed," he said softly, lifting her hand to his mouth. "Are you sure you won't reconsider having an affair with me? I'm yours for the asking, you know."

She laughed lightly, genuinely amused, despite her concern at what they may find in a few minutes. "I'll let you know if I change my mind," she told him.

"You do that," he replied. Then he kissed her knuckles again and placed her hand back in her lap.

Spring turned her head to look out the window beside her, but her thoughts were not on the passing scenery. Instead, she thought of Clay. She liked him.

She really liked him. She liked his melting smile, his offbeat humor and his obvious sensitivity. She liked his blue-green eyes, his golden hair and the pleasure he seemed to find in the most casual of touches. She was even beginning to like the way he dressed. Now *that* should have been frightening. Yet somehow it wasn't.

Broadway, with its strip joints and businesses catering to every prurient interest, had been Spring's least favorite part of the quick sight-seeing tour of San Francisco that Summer had given her the day before. Clay took her into an area that Summer had avoided altogether. He parked in front of a crumbling dump of a building that should have been condemned years earlier, and probably had been. The littered street was completely deserted in the bright afternoon sunlight, but Spring suspected that the shadows of evening would bring out all the human flotsam that would inhabit such a place. She shivered, thinking of a lonely fifteen-year-old girl. "This is where she is?"

Looking grim, Clay tugged at his tweed cap. "That's what I was told."

Something in his posture told her that he wasn't telling her everything he'd heard. She only hoped she would be able to help him. Following his lead, she took a deep breath and climbed from the car. She noticed that his eyes, no longer smiling, darted all around them as they entered the dark, unwelcoming building through a door that had long since ceased to lock or even close properly. Clay walked unerringly to a flight of bare metal stairs. "Up here," he told Spring.

She hesitated for only a moment. He reached out and took her hand. Strengthened by the contact, she nodded at him and walked just behind him up two flights to the third floor, the top floor of the building. Clay looked around for a moment, seemed to get his bearings, then led her down a hallway to their left, never releasing her hand, for which Spring was grateful. At the end of the hallway was a closed door. Clay stood for a moment before it, then knocked tentatively. "Thelma? It's Clay. Are you there?"

When no answer came from the other side of the door, Clay knocked louder. "Thelma? Come on, sweetheart, let me in. I only want to talk, to make sure you're okay. Can you hear me?"

Again, silence. Clay looked at Spring, then at the doorknob. Still holding her hand, he twisted the rusted metal knob. The door wasn't locked. It opened with a screech of angry hinges.

The smells struck her first. She didn't know what they were, nor did she want to. Her eyes were focused on the teenager sprawled on a filthy bare mattress that lay on the trash-covered floor. The girl wasn't moving. Spring was horribly afraid that she was dead.

Clay was already across the room, down on one knee in the dirt as he touched Thelma's face. He looked up at Spring, his face as expressionless as if carved of stone. "She's burning up with fever. She's very ill."

"Do you know what's wrong with her?"

"No. Flu, maybe, or pneumonia. God knows when she ate last. I was told by one of her friends that she wasn't well when she disappeared. Her mother was mad at her for missing a couple of days at her after-school job in a fast-food restaurant. Thelma's tiny salary is more important to her mother than Thelma is, it seems." Dull fury glinted in Clay's eyes, making them seem suddenly hard, without a trace of his usual laughter.

"I'll find a phone," Spring told him, moving backward.

"No." The harsh, flat syllable stopped her. "I don't want you out on those streets. I'll go. Do you mind staying with her?"

"Of course not."

Clay touched her shoulder in passing. She could feel the fine trembling in his fingers. He paused at the doorway. "You'll be okay? You're not frightened? I won't be long."

"I'm fine," Spring assured him. "Hurry, Clay. She looks so ill."

He ground out a curse between clenched teeth and ran.

Left alone with the unconscious teenager, Spring breathed deeply for courage, then almost gagged as the rank odors assaulted her again. She took Thelma's limp hand in hers, fingers closing around the thin brown wrist to monitor the reedy pulse. She's just a child, she thought, looking down at the vulnerable face. She'd been told Thelma was fifteen; she would never have guessed so from looking at her. Thelma's hair, which was now badly in need of washing, was cut to curl around her head. Long eyelashes lay on soft, full cheeks that would normally be a rich chocolate but were now ashen. Her mouth was a child's mouth, tender and full, open to expose even white teeth. Spring felt her heart twist in her chest. She eyed the girl's dirty sweatshirt and torn, faded jeans and blinked back tears. "Don't worry, Thelma. You're going to be just fine," she murmured, though she doubted that her words registered.

Thelma's breathing was labored and harsh, punctuated by a hacking cough, her skin hot and dry. Spring wished fervently that she had a cool, wet cloth to wash

Thelma's face. Then she reached eagerly for the small handbag hanging from her shoulder and dug into it, coming up with one of the packaged moistened paper napkins provided by some fast-food establishments. For once she was grateful for her habit of saving possibly useful odds and ends. She ripped open the foil package, gratefully breathing in the lemony scent before gently placing it against Thelma's face, talking softly and soothingly. She thought she saw Thelma's eyes open once, briefly, but there was no other sign that she was aware of anything going on around her.

Clay found Spring that way, on her knees beside the mattress, heedless of the dirt being ground into her light-colored jeans, tenderly bathing the face of a sick young woman she'd never laid eyes on before. He was struck by Spring's quiet strength. A lot of women would have run shuddering from the room, afraid to be exposed to whatever germs were rampant here. But not Spring. He moved over beside her, dropping an arm around her shoulders. "I'm sure that feels good to her."

Spring looked around at him. "It was all I had."

"It'll do. The ambulance will be here soon."

"She's barely stirred. Is she . . . do you think she's in a coma?"

"I don't know, Spring. I don't know what—or even if—she's eaten since she disappeared nine days ago. I think she's had a friend with her some, but the other kid's even younger than Thelma and not capable of dealing with the situation. She'd promised Thelma not to tell where she was, but she got scared and broke down when Frank questioned her."

The ambulance team arrived then, bearing a stretcher. Spring thought she'd never seen two more beautiful people in her life.

"You okay?" Clay had his arms around her as she stood weakly, watching the medical team going efficiently about its business of saving Thelma's life.

She leaned her head into his shoulder. "Yes. Clay, do you think she's going to make it?"

"I don't know, Spring. I just don't know."

The two paramedics already had Thelma on the stretcher. Together they lifted her, her slight weight giving them little resistance.

"We'll follow them to the hospital," Clay told Spring, leading her to the door with one arm still tightly around her shoulders. "I have to know that she gets there all right."

"Of course." She would have expected no less. She would have allowed no less.

Thelma made it to the hospital alive. The doctors could make no promises that she would remain that way. She was diagnosed as having a severe case of viral pneumonia, complicated by various secondary infections probably caused by exposure and malnourishment. Clay called Thelma's mother, coming back to the waiting room with his face hard and his eyes angry. Spring had never seen him angry. "We'll stay until that . . . woman gets here," he told her. "Then I'll have to leave. I won't be able to stay in the same hospital with her without losing my cool completely."

It wasn't long before Mrs. Sawyer arrived, loudly blaming her daughter, Clay, Thelma's friends—everyone but herself—for Thelma's problems. True to his word, Clay left the hospital almost immediately, visibly restraining himself from giving vent to his anger. In his car he sat immobile behind the steering wheel, staring out the windshield at the hospital.

"Are you all right?" Spring asked tentatively, wanting to reach out to him but not knowing how. She laced her fingers in her lap, noting impassively that they were dirty.

He inhaled deeply and turned his head to look at her. "Yeah," he answered, "but it makes me so damned mad."

"I know," she told him softly.

Not as shy as she was about reaching out, Clay took her hand, dirt and all, and squeezed it. "You were wonderful. I don't know how to thank you."

"You don't have to," she told him, flushing slightly. "I didn't do it for you."

He smiled, though weakly. "No, you didn't, did you? You did it for Thelma. A kid you don't even know."

Embarrassed by his praise, she looked away. "How long do you plan to stay in this parking lot?" she demanded a bit huskily.

In answer he started the car. Backing out of the parking space, he asked, "Okay with you if we go by my place? I'd like to clean up before I take you back to your sister's. I'm filthy."

Of course she told him that she didn't mind at all, though the thought of being alone with him in his home made her swallow hard. She'd seen a different side of Clay this afternoon, a side she found much too fascinating. And even with dirt streaked across one cheek and smeared liberally on his worn jeans, he was too damned attractive for her peace of mind.

She fell in love with his house. One of the Victorians that added to San Francisco's quaint charm, it sat regal and arrogant, wearing its bright blue paint and funny little stained-glass windows with studied nonchalance. It reminded her a lot of Clay. "It's wonderful," she told him sincerely, even as she found herself wondering how he could afford such a choice piece of San Francisco real estate. He had a doctorate degree in counseling, but he worked in the public-school system, didn't he? Then she told herself that Clay's finances were none of her business. After all, they were only passing acquaintances, she reminded herself sternly.

He smiled broadly, not bothering to hide his deep pleasure at her praise. "You're not the only one who's into restoring old homes," he commented, subtly pointing out another thing they had in common. "I've been working on the inside for a couple of years. It's almost finished."

He led her in and allowed her to look around without asking for comment. She loved it. All the clever nooks and crannies, the elegant, just slightly eccentric antique and reproduction Victorian furnishings that again were so typical of Clay. A shiver coursed down her spine at the strange similarity in their taste in furnishings. Clay had some pieces that were almost identical to ones that were even now residing in her apartment in Little Rock!

She loved it, she thought again. And then she made a deliberate attempt to wipe the word "love" from her mind as she turned back to the handsome blonde tagging at her heels. For some reason it made her nervous. "Beautiful," she summed up succinctly.

"Me or the house?" he demanded cockily, some of his bold self-assurance returning now that they'd put the hospital behind them.

"Both of you," she answered with a sigh. "You said something about cleaning up?"

He wasn't quite sure how to take her unexpected answer, so he ignored it. "Yes, I would like to shower and change. I'll be quick. I could dig you up something to wear if you want to shower, as well."

Spring looked down at her aqua jeans, streaked with greasy dirt from the floor in that little room where she'd knelt by Thelma. Her brow creased into a frown.

"Spring? What's wrong?"

"Are there many kids who live that way?" she whispered, her violet eyes huge behind her smudged glasses. "All that filth . . ."

Clay released a long, weary breath. "Believe it or not, I've seen worse than what we found this afternoon. The streets are full of runaways, easy prey for every sleaze bag and drug dealer in town. Teenagers with unhappy homes migrate toward California, New York and Florida by the thousands. Too many for the authorities to handle, and the shelters available are sadly inadequate."

"Do you work much with runaways?"

"Some. Mostly I deal with the kids who are having problems at home, before they run. I try to prevent them from turning to the streets."

"I can see why Summer has joined your cause," Spring murmured. "It's heart wrenching to see a child like Thelma was today, when she should be hanging out at McDonald's, laughing and flirting with nice boys her age. It makes me wish there was something *I* could do to help."

"We can always use another volunteer," Clay told her, watching her more closely than his teasing tone seemed to warrant.

She forced a weak smile. "Maybe I'll look into it when I get back to Little Rock. There may be a Halloran House there in need of an optometrist's spare time."

Clay frowned at her mention of returning to Little Rock. Why the sudden hollow feeling? he asked himself. Surely he hadn't forgotten that she was here for less than two weeks. Without stopping to think about it he reached out and pulled her into his arms, ignoring that both of them were dirty. He hugged her tightly. "I'm glad you went with me," he said huskily.

She stirred restlessly in his embrace, aware of a desire to put her arms around him and return it. "I didn't help much," she protested. "I just did what had to be done."

"Always the brave, responsible big sister," Clay murmured, thinking of things Summer had told him about Spring. "It wasn't easy being the oldest, was it?"

She frowned a little, wondering what her childhood had to do with what had happened that afternoon, what was happening now. "I don't know what you mean."

He chuckled softly, reaching down to lift her chin so that he was gazing directly into her eyes through her smudged glasses. "You do what has to be done," he said simply. "You have this sense of responsibility that seems to give you strength that many people lack. Like this afternoon, you didn't panic when we found Thelma in such terrible shape. You didn't scold me for taking you into that situation or leaving you alone with her while I called an ambulance. You just calmly took care of her."

"I wasn't all that calm."

"No, but you hid your qualms long enough to do what had to be done. Thanks, love."

Love. There was that word again. She reminded herself that Clay was a demonstrative man, to whom such casual endearments were second nature.

Slowly, reluctantly, she eased herself from his embrace. "Yes, well," she faltered, not quite meeting his eyes. "Why don't you go ahead and take your shower?"

"I will. And you? My offer's still open for you to take one, too."

"No, I'll just wash up. I can shower when you take me back to Summer's. Thanks, anyway."

"Okay. The guest bath is down this hall on the left. I'll be in the bath in the master bedroom if you need anything. Or if you suddenly get an urge to wash my back," he added audaciously, wanting to see her smile again.

The smile broke loose despite her efforts to hold it back. "You're a big boy, Clay. I'm sure you can manage to wash yourself."

"Someday, Spring Reed, you are going to offer to wash my back," Clay told her, leaning over to kiss her before he pulled away and headed toward his bedroom.

"Don't hold your breath," Spring shot after him, then wished she'd come up with something more original. She heard his chuckle as he disappeared down the long, wallpapered hallway in the opposite direction of the bathroom he'd indicated for her.

4

SPRING CLEANED UP as best she could, washing her face and hands and reapplying a touch of makeup from the items she carried in her purse. She brushed out her hair and twisted it back into its customary knot. Her clothes were still soiled and disheveled, but at least she felt a bit fresher. She wouldn't have been comfortable showering or changing into anything belonging to Clay. Or were there women's clothes hanging somewhere in his house? Perhaps that's what he'd meant by offering to find her something to wear.

She tried to tell herself that she was suddenly depressed only because of all that had happened during the past few hours.

Spring was waiting in the living room when Clay joined her. She inhaled sharply at the sight of him. His hair lay in damp curls around his face, gleaming dull gold and almost crying out to be touched. His skin glowed from his hot shower, and his eyes were brighter and bluer than she'd ever seen them. He had pulled on a pale yellow cotton crewneck sweater and dark brown slacks that hugged his lean hips. Barefoot, he carried brown TOPSIDERS in one hand. "Don't you ever wear socks?" she demanded, because she had to say something and nothing else came to mind just then. Nothing she cared to say out loud, anyway.

"No, I never wear socks. Don't you ever wear your hair down?" he returned, lifting a hand to touch her neatly twisted tresses.

"Not very often. It gets in my way."

"Then why haven't you cut it short, the way Summer wears hers?"

"Because I look funny with short hair," she answered with a shrug.

He laughed softly. "Or could it be that inside that practical, responsible exterior is a secret romantic who likes long hair?"

"Don't be ridiculous," she replied, annoyed. "Would you mind taking me back to Summer's now? I would really like to change into clean clothes."

"I offered you some of mine."

"I doubt that you would have anything my size," she said, her words a challenge.

"About the best I could offer is a sweatshirt and sweatpants," he agreed. "They'd be clean, but I can't guarantee fit. Afraid I don't keep women's clothes around." His words answered her challenge.

"Yes, well, I'll be fine until I can change into my own clothes," she muttered, suddenly uncomfortable. She picked up her purse and tucked it under her arm.

"Wait a minute." Clay slid his feet into his shoes, then walked toward her, stopping only a few inches away from her. "I wanted to thank you again for what you did this afternoon."

She shifted on her feet. "You've already thanked me. Repeatedly."

"Not properly," he murmured. Very deliberately he removed her glasses, folded them and dropped them into the outside pocket of her purse as she stood watching him, making no effort to move away. "Let me thank you properly, Spring." And he lowered his mouth to hers, slowly, giving her plenty of time to draw back.

She stayed where she was, her lips parting just as his touched them. She closed her eyes, blocking out the sight of his devastating face, blocking out reason, locking in sensation. His kiss was that of an experienced lover, thorough and deep and sure. She was trembling when it ended, and he had touched her with no more than his mouth. He drew back only an inch or so, took one long look at her expression, then groaned and pulled her into his arms.

The second kiss was just as thorough, just as deep, but not quite as sure. For some reason Spring thought that Clay seemed less polished this time, guided more by passion than practice. She could feel the unsteadiness of his arms around her. It would have been hard to resist him before. It was impossible now.

Neither of them noticed when her purse hit the floor at her feet. They both noticed when her arms went around his neck, pressing her full length against him. Their moans were simultaneous, aroused. Spring allowed her head to fall back, deepening the kiss. Clay swept her slender body with his hands, learning her curves, seeking out the hollow of her spine, finally pressing inward to hold her against his thighs.

Hard. He was so hard—his arms muscled from whatever sport he regularly played, his chest solid and plated where her breasts were flattened against it. Hard where his arousal boldly made itself felt against her abdomen. Yet his mouth over hers, the golden hair at his nape where her fingers burrowed were soft. So soft. She wanted to explore every inch of him, to kiss every soft spot, stroke every hard one. She wanted him.

Emotions that were already strained from the stress of the afternoon flared into desire so hot, so intense that it shook both of them. Clay didn't know whether the shudder had been hers or his or mutual. He only knew that he wanted her, needed her, as he'd never wanted or needed before. Her fiery response to his kiss was driving him mad. How could he have known that such demanding passion smoldered beneath her proper, almost prim appearance? He was delighted with the discovery. He wanted more.

"Spring," he muttered, raising his hands to cradle her face as he continued to caress her with slanting, nibbling kisses. Nothing more. Just her name. He had needed to say it.

"Oh, Clay," she breathed without opening her eyes, her hands sliding around to rest against his chest. Her fingers splayed, then curled, kneading the taut skin beneath the soft sweater.

"Look at me, Spring."

Almost shyly her lashes fluttered upward. Even slightly blurred by her myopia, his face was so beautiful. "It's not fair," she murmured, speaking to herself.

"What's not fair, sweetheart?"

"That you should look like this," she answered incautiously, touching her fingertips to his tanned cheek. "That you should make me feel this way."

"I could say the same about you," he replied, nuzzling her cheek. "You're so lovely. And you make me crazy."

"Oh, God, what am I doing?" She dropped her hand and stepped back, crossing her arms at her waist in unconscious defensiveness. "Take me back to Sausalito, Clay."

"The only place I want to take you is upstairs to my bedroom," he told her unsteadily. "I want to make love to you for hours, until you're too weak to move. And then I want to start all over again."

Her heart pounded, her mind filled with tantalizing images, but she held tightly to reason. "No, Clay."

He exhaled gustily, shoving fingers that were still not quite steady through his rumpled hair. "Okay, we'll wait until you're ready. But the time *will* come, Spring. It's inevitable."

"No, it won't," she returned with admirable confidence. "I won't let it."

He wanted to argue, to demand her reasons for holding back when they both knew she wanted him as badly as he wanted her. He wanted to pick her up in his arms and sweep aside all her objections in a flurry of kisses. But he only reached down to retrieve her purse from where it had fallen on the tapestry carpet and hold it out to her. She had her reasons. She would share them with him when she was ready. He had to make sure she was ready soon, before she left California and the opportunity to make love with her was lost.

He stayed only a short time at the Anderson home, just long enough to tell Summer what had happened and thoroughly embarrass Spring with his lavish praise. He left with the excuse that he was going to see what he could do for Thelma. Just before he walked out, he gathered Spring into his arms and kissed her hard, right in front of Summer and Derek. Her face was stained a vivid scarlet when he left her with a cocky grin and a promise to pick her up the next evening for their date.

"*Don't* say it," Spring warned Summer the moment the door had closed behind Clay.

"You must be hungry, Spring," Derek interceded quickly. "I'll go put some steaks on the grill. How do you like yours?"

"Medium," she replied, still glaring at her giggling sister.

Derek made a prudent, hasty escape.

"If you could have seen your face," Summer murmured, her blue eyes dancing. "You should know Clay well enough by now to realize that he has no regard for spectators."

"How long have you known that man?" Spring demanded, ignoring Summer's comment.

"I met him soon after I moved to San Francisco. I'd found a job working as a hostess in an elegant little restaurant near Nob Hill. Not exactly my style, but it paid the rent on the tiny apartment I'd found. I didn't know many people and I was lonely, though I'd started to make a few friends here and there. Then one night Clay came into the restaurant with a date. I couldn't help but watch them. He was so gorgeous—"

"I've noticed," Spring muttered.

Summer ignored her. "And his date was drop-dead beautiful. Tall brunette with coal-black eyes and a figure that would make most women want to sob."

Spring found that she really didn't want to hear Summer's description, but she continued to listen in reluctant fascination.

"Anyway, the woman bitched from the time she walked into the place. I don't know what her problem was that evening or why Clay was out with her in the first place, but she was a real honey. They had to wait to be seated because Clay had forgotten to make reservations, which didn't exactly go over with his date. I caught his eye a few times and tried to look sympathetic, and then, all of a sudden, he and I started laughing. Once we got started, it was hard to stop. The wicked witch got all huffy and walked out, refusing to let Clay take her home, though to give him credit he tried. So he stayed and had dinner alone, and by the time he left, he and I had a date for the next evening."

"You went out with him?" Spring frowned, disturbed at the thought. Was Clay still attracted to Summer, despite her being married to someone else?

"Yes, we went out. By the end of our first date, we were the best of friends and we knew that's all we'd ever be. We've been the best of friends ever since. He's a very special man, Spring."

Spring looked down at her lap, rubbing at a streak of dirt with one fingertip. "I'm sure he is. He seems very committed to his young people."

"Oh, he is. He makes a big difference in their lives. He's also a good friend, always willing to offer a shoulder or a hand when he's needed. He hasn't had an easy life, but he never lost his sense of humor."

"Why wasn't his life easy?" Spring asked curiously.

"Clay was one of those troubled kids that he works with now. A real hard case. Ran away, got into trouble, came much too close to drugs and other illegal activities. He ended up in a home for incorrigible teenagers, where—fortunately—he was able to turn himself around with help from some very good counselors."

That explained a lot about the man. Spring frowned as she thought over what Summer had told her. "Didn't his family try to help him?"

"His family was his problem. Very old-money. Snobs who cared more about having a 'perfect' child than a happy one. He was ignored when he was good, vi-

ciously criticized when he wasn't. It's no wonder he re-
belled."

"He was an only child?" Spring asked, her tender
heart twisting at the story. She would never have imagined that happy-go-lucky Clay had come from such an
unhappy background.

"Yes. He inherited a near fortune when his parents
died a few years ago. Still, he works as a school counselor and lives pretty much on his salary. Other than
his weakness for his house and his sports car and his
crazy clothes, Clay uses his money mostly to help the
less fortunate."

"As you said, a very special man," Spring murmured.

Summer shrugged. "He's not perfect, of course, but
then, he never wanted to be. He only wants to be accepted for what he is. Now about that kiss—"

"The steaks are ready," Derek announced from the
doorway, much to Spring's relief. "Summer-love, why
don't you bring out the salad you made earlier?"

Spring shot him a grateful smile, her mind full with
everything that had happened to her and everything
that she had learned that day. She excused herself to
change into clean clothes before dinner, and not once
did Clay McEntire leave her mind.

AFTER A LEISURELY BREAKFAST Monday morning, Derek
left for his office and Summer for her college class, both
encouraging Spring to make herself at home. Summer
had only morning classes that day and would be home
by lunch, she promised. Derek planned to come home
for lunch, as well. Spring waved them off, then indulged in a lazy swim in the temperature-regulated

pool. She felt almost decadent enjoying such leisure after the hard pace she'd sustained at home for so long.

After her swim she took a long, hot shower. Her skin was glowing bright pink by the time she stepped out and reached for a fluffy towel. Her reflection in a mirror caught her eye, and she paused, staring thoughtfully at her nude image. A bit too slim, she thought critically, but not bad on the whole. Would Clay find her appealing if he should see her this way?

Realizing the direction her thoughts were taking, she snatched up the towel and applied it furiously. Deep within herself she was aware of a faint sense of regret that she wasn't the type who could cheerfully indulge in a teeth-rattling vacation affair and then just walk away. If she were, Clay would definitely be the man she'd choose for her fling. As it was, he was the man she most needed to resist.

Lunch was a scrumptious seafood salad prepared by Spring. She had the food ready by the time Derek and Summer arrived, and they took their time over the meal, chatting contentedly. They'd just finished eating when the telephone rang. Derek answered, listened for a moment, laughed, then extended the receiver in Spring's direction. "For you," he told her.

She knew who it was by the glint in her brother-in-law's eyes. Taking a deep breath, she accepted the phone and pressed it to her ear. "Hello, Clay."

"Hi, sweet Spring. Oh, sorry. I'm not supposed to call you that, am I?"

"No," she answered sternly. "You're not. Aren't you supposed to be working?"

"Taking a break. I'm calling from my office."

"Oh. Have you heard anything about Thelma?"

"No change," he replied, immediately serious. "She should have been hospitalized days ago. She had to have surgery this morning to remove the fluid that has built up in her lungs. The membranes had become infected. They have her in intensive care now."

"I'm sorry."

"Yeah." He paused for a moment, then deliberately lightened his tone. "Actually, I was calling to remind you about our date tonight. You haven't forgotten, have you?"

"No, Clay, I haven't forgotten."

"Great. I'm really looking forward to it. How about you?"

She pressed her tongue firmly against her cheek, then replied with mock gravity, "I'm sure it will be quite pleasant. There's nothing interesting on television tonight, anyway."

Clay seemed to choke on the other end of the line, then growled, "Talk about damning with faint praise. I owe you for that one, sweet Spring." He tacked on the nickname with deliberate challenge.

She refused to take him up on it. "I'll see you tonight, Clay."

"Okay. Oh, and, Spring."

"Yes?"

"Dress funky."

She frowned. "Funky?"

"Yeah, funky. For you I guess that means leaving the top button of your silk blouse undone. See you tonight."

Spring stared for a moment at the buzzing receiver in her hand, then slowly replaced it on its cradle. "Your friend," she told her avidly interested sister, "is a lunatic."

Summer laughed. "Yes, I know."

"He wants me to dress funky tonight."

"So what are you going to do about it?" Summer asked, the words a dare.

Spring grinned and turned her gaze to her bemused brother-in-law. "Derek, dear, how do you feel about loaning out your clothes?" she asked blandly.

Her family would have immediately recognized the look on Spring's pretty face. She didn't often indulge her sly, subtle sense of humor, but when she did, the results were never predictable. Being a new member of the family, Derek wasn't quite sure how to interpret the gleam in Spring's violet eyes. Having twenty-five years of experience behind her, Summer identified it immediately. She suspected that her own wardrobe was about to be raided and that a quick shopping excursion might even be in order. She laughed again and looked forward to the evening, immensely pleased with the unexpected developments taking place during her sister's visit.

CLAY STOOD on the doorstep of the Anderson home and checked his appearance, as anxious as a schoolboy on his first date, he mused ruefully. He thoughtfully twisted one foot in front of him, wondering if the orange high-tops clashed too badly with his tan three-piece suit and brown-on-beige striped dress shirt. He checked the knot in the mottled brown-and-green tie that he'd tucked discreetly into his buttoned vest. He'd worn his favorite tie in Spring's honor.

He chuckled as he punched the doorbell, wondering if Spring had taken his advice about how to dress. He could almost picture her now in the neat little suit she'd probably chosen to wear like a coat of mail while with him.

Summer's giggle when she opened the door and eyed his attire tipped him off that something was up. He grinned, eagerly looking for his date. His grin widened when he found her. She *had* dressed funky.

He slowly examined her from head to toe. A gray felt fedora sat atop her light hair, which she wore in a glorious frizz to her shoulders. A loose, unstructured charcoal-gray linen jacket that Clay had helped Summer select as a gift for Derek was pushed up to Spring's elbows and hung almost to her knees. Her bright pink blouse was open at the collar so that the man's pink-and-gray spotted silk tie was knotted at about the middle of her chest. Light gray slacks were pleated baggily at her slender waist, narrowing from the knees to tightly grip her ankles. Her feet were tied into heeled black lace-up half-boots. She wore enormous turquoise-and-silver earrings, a chunky matching choker and a thick black leather belt with a gaudy silver-and-turquoise buckle. Facing him with a smile that contained equal parts of shyness and bravado, she looked beautiful.

"I am in love with this woman," he remarked aloud, almost as if he were commenting on the weather. And he knew his words were the truth. He watched in amusement as her face turned almost as pink as her shirt.

"I thought you said you were going to dress funky," Spring accused him.

He frowned down at his suit. "I *am* dressed funky."

"Spring, he's wearing a *tie*," Summer pointed out with a grin. "The only part of his outfit that's *not* funky, for Clay, is the tennis shoes."

Spring shook her head, causing her crimped curls to sway around her face. "San Francisco," she muttered, then glared at Clay. "Okay, let's go."

He couldn't resist throwing an arm around her shoulders and giving her one hard hug. "We're going to have so much fun!" he told her cheerfully.

"Yeah," she answered with a resigned sigh that he found greatly amusing. "Fun."

THE PLAY THAT CLAY TOOK her to turned out to be a junior-high-school production of *You Can't Take It With You*, which happened to be one of Spring's favorite plays. She didn't tell him so. Nor did she give in to the impulse to tease him when she noticed him squinting a bit as he read the program, though her professional mind made a note to ask him later if he'd had an eye examination recently.

Instead, she sat back and enjoyed, chuckling at the more-enthusiastic-than-talented performances from the young teenage actors. Or, rather, she appeared to enjoy the play. It wasn't easy with Clay sitting close beside her, taking advantage of every opportunity to touch her. When he wasn't patting her arm, he was squeezing her knee. As the performance went on, the squeezes moved gradually up her thigh until, at the beginning of act three, she was forced to catch his hand and return it firmly to his own lap. She tried very hard to look as if his touches annoyed her, when actually they turned her into Silly Putty.

With admirably few forgotten or blown lines Alice and Tony pledged their undying love, Grandpa Vanderhof congratulated himself on outsmarting the government, Penelope and Paul Sycamore went on with their happy, eccentric lives and the play ended. Spring

applauded warmly as the flushed young actors took
their bows.

"Want to go backstage?" Clay asked, draping a casual arm around Spring's shoulders.

"You know someone in the cast?" she inquired with
interest.

He nodded noncommittally and led her down the
aisle, never breaking physical contact. Though she told
herself that she wished he'd stop touching her, Spring
was fully aware that she made no effort to pull away
from him.

To say that Clay knew someone in the cast was a
monumental understatement. Clay knew *everyone* in
the cast. And they quite obviously idolized him. For-
bidden by school policy to call him by his first name—
this was the very school where he worked, Spring discovered—they called him Mr. Mac. They teased him
about his unusually conservative clothing, glowed with
pride when he congratulated them on the success of
their performances and competed avidly for his attention. The boys all tried to emulate him. The girls were
all in love with him. Watching him with the kids, Spring
felt herself slipping into a similar infatuation.

When Clay introduced her to the cast, Spring was
glad she'd dressed so oddly, though she'd chosen her
"funky" outfit just to prove to Clay that she wasn't as
prim and humorless as he'd teased her about being. The
kids seemed to accept her easily as his friend, even
showing their implicit approval by teasing her about
her Arkansan accent.

Declaring himself to be near starvation, Clay took
her out to eat when they left the school. The tiny Italian restaurant he selected was tucked away in an ob-
scure section of the city, far from the usual tourist paths.

Lulled by the pleasant evening and marvelous food, Spring found herself chattering easily, more comfortable on a date than she'd been in a long time. Clay stayed on his best behavior, seemingly fascinated with stories of her childhood in Rose Bud and her optometry practice in Little Rock. Conversation turned to mutual interests, and Clay grinned more broadly each time they found something in common—favorite books, movies, music, television programs.

"It's Kismet," he declared at one point. "Our tastes are so similar. There's absolutely no reason not to have an affair."

She shook her head reprovingly at him, taking his words as a joke. "What about our taste in clothes?"

"What about it? You look great tonight."

"But I don't look like *me* tonight. I only wore these things to surprise you."

"I know you did. But I like the way you dress when you're being yourself, too. Your prim little outfits dare a man to rip them off you."

He laughed when she blushed vividly.

"The least you could have done," she complained, struggling to keep up with him, "was to dress in your usual outrageous manner after asking me to go funky. You look so... so *normal* in that suit. And it really wasn't necessary to wear a tie to a junior-high-school play."

He looked crestfallen, though his eyes twinkled with secret amusement. "Don't you like Morgan?"

She lifted a questioning eyebrow. "Morgan?"

"My tie."

"You *named* your tie? Clay, people don't name their ties."

"I do. He's named after the friend who gave him to me."

She continued to look at him as though he were crazy—which, of course, pretty well summed up her opinion of him. Gorgeous, sexy, mesmerizing, but un-questionably crazy. "Your tie is a him?"

"Looks like a him to me," he answered reflectively, tugging the end of the tie out of his vest and smoothing it downward so that she could see its full length. "Don't you think so?"

Spring choked, then burst into laughter. "Oh, my God. Your tie is a *fish!*" Fully exposed, the mottled browns and greens became scales. The fish-shaped tie was cleverly designed, the end a fish-head profile, complete with gills, closed mouth and one glassy blue eye. "That's disgusting."

Her laughter had brought an odd light to his eyes. Smiling at her in a manner that she couldn't begin to interpret—nor did she care to try just then—he reached across the table to take her hand. "I knew you'd appreciate Morgan."

They talked of his work, both at the school and with the young people he continually referred to as "my kids" at Halloran House. Spring was fascinated by his dedication to the youth, his understanding of them and the way their minds worked.

"Do many of them run away from home?" she asked, thinking of Thelma.

"It happens often enough," he answered regretfully. "I'm afraid I was a runaway myself a few times. I know how cold and lonely it can be out on the streets." He had told her a bit about his childhood during dinner, an abbreviated version of what Summer had already told her.

"I always feel so sorry for the parents. Not to know where their children are, wondering if they're dead or alive, and all usually because of a simple breakdown in communications."

"It's sad for everyone concerned," Clay agreed. "Sometimes the parents couldn't care less what happens to the kids, but I know that's not always true. Many times the problems can be remedied through family therapy, once they realize that they need help—not that the problems are ever simple."

Spring thought that perhaps Clay would tend to be biased toward the young people's side in any family encounter, but considering his background and his vocation, she supposed that was understandable. She deliberately turned the conversation to lighter subjects, not wanting Clay to dwell on his career just then.

She was almost disappointed when he drove her straight back to Summer's house after dinner, though she didn't know exactly where she'd wanted him to take her. She only knew that she wasn't ready to say goodnight to him.

Clay parked the car in the driveway, snapped off the lights and turned to Spring, one arm over the back of his seat as he smiled at her. "I had fun tonight, Spring. Thanks for going with me."

She moistened her lips and returned the smile. He looked so good in the shadowy artificial light from outside. But then, he looked good in broad daylight, also. Or any kind of light. "I had fun, too. Thank you."

He chuckled, his hand stretching out to twist one of her curls. "Aren't we being polite?"

Because she was fighting the urge to catch his hand and hold it to her cheek, her own smile was a bit forced. "Yes, aren't we?"

Something in her expression must have given away her feelings, for his smile slowly faded, to be replaced by a look of hunger that matched hers. "I'd like to kiss you, Spring," he murmured, his hand sliding into the hair at her temple to cradle her face. "I think I want to kiss you now more than I've ever wanted to do anything in my life."

5

SINCE WHEN HAD HE STARTED asking permission to kiss her? She wet her lips again, realizing nervously that he wanted more than startled acceptance this time. He wanted full cooperation. He was making an implicit demand for her to acknowledge that she was attracted to him, that she wanted the kiss as badly as he did. Even as she almost shyly removed her glasses and leaned toward him, she wondered how much more he would force her to admit.

Her lips had barely touched his before he was kissing her. The battered fedora tumbled off her head, unnoticed by either of them. His mouth slanted greedily over hers, moving with the same rough-gentle passion with which he'd kissed her the day before. And, as with the last time, she could only hold on and allow herself to be lost in him. A far distant part of her mind pondered her response to him. She'd never been like this with anyone else. She'd never relinquished control. Clay took her control, yet he seemed no more the master of his own emotions than she was of hers.

It felt only natural when his hand slipped beneath her borrowed, oversize jacket to settle with bold possessiveness on one of her breasts. Almost unconsciously she inhaled, pushing herself more fully into his touch.

"Ah, God, Spring. You feel so good in my arms." His voice was only a breath against her lips; he refused to break the contact between them.

She didn't know what to say except his name. It seemed to be enough. He kissed her again, and this time his tongue surged between her lips to caress hers. Teasingly. Tenderly. Lovingly.

"Kiss me back, sweetheart," he muttered, then took her mouth again.

With no further hesitation she gave in to his half-pleading demand and returned his kiss with all the formerly unknown passion within her.

After what seemed like a hot, life-altering eternity, Clay suddenly startled her by pulling his mouth away from hers, giving a low, husky laugh and hugging her with such fervent enthusiasm that she thought she would have at least a few bruises, if not broken bones, when he released her. "You never stop surprising me, Spring Reed," he told her with apparent delight. "We're going to be so good together."

She swallowed hard. "We're . . . what?"

Cradling her face in his hands, he smiled meltingly at her and kissed her nose. "When we make love, it's going to be the most exquisite, most erotic, most incredible thing that has ever happened to either of us. I can hardly wait."

That got her attention. Spring backed frantically away from him, pressing herself uncomfortably against the door behind her. "I've already told you, Clay, we are *not* going to have an affair."

Flashing his most boyishly charming grin, Clay grabbed the hand that was pushing forcefully against his chest and kissed her knuckles. "We're already having an affair, Spring. We just haven't made love yet."

"Nor will we," she snapped, jerking her hand out of his and shoving it shakily through her tangled hair. Summer's hat. She couldn't find the hat. She looked wildly around for it, talking rapidly as she grabbed her purse and the borrowed fedora and held them protectively against her breasts. "What happened just now was a mistake. I can't—I won't let it happen again."

"It will happen again." Clay spoke almost lazily as he watched her frantic preparations for escape with visible amusement. "Again and again and again, until you admit that it's utterly ridiculous to try to deny this thing that's between us. You can call it love or lust or earth-shaking attraction, but it's there, and it's not going to go away."

"Then we'll just have to ignore it," she declared. *Call it love*, he had said. No. She wouldn't call it love.

"Can't you see that this won't work, Clay?" She was almost pleading now. "I'm just not the type who can handle this sort of thing. Please don't ask for something I can't give."

His face softened and took on an expression of such sweetness that it brought a lump to her throat. He touched her cheek, fleetingly, not enough to force her to draw back again. "Darling, you've already given it. You just haven't admitted it yet."

Given what? Her heart? "No, Clay," she whispered, shaking her head.

He knew when to quit—temporarily. "I'll walk you to the door."

Before she could protest, he was out of the car and at her side as she walked in awkward silence to the front door of her sister's home. She used the key that Summer had given her, then paused with one hand on the doorknob. "Clay, I—"

He silenced her with a quick kiss on her slightly swollen lips. "Good night, Spring. You'll be seeing me around in the next few days. A lot."

Threat or promise, the words held a note of determination that she had to take seriously. Without giving her a chance to reply, Clay whirled on one orange tennis shoe and left her staring after him.

THIRTY MINUTES LATER Spring stood before the mirror in her bedroom, brushing out her hair as Summer sat cross-legged on the bed, her compact body almost quivering with frustration. "Aren't you going to tell me anything about your date with Clay?" Summer demanded, her elbows on her knees as she stared at her sister's reflection.

"I told you it was nice."

Summer snorted inelegantly. "*Nice.* Yuck."

Spring set down her brush and turned, tightening the sash of her pastel flowered robe. "What's wrong with nice?"

"It's insipid. It's something you'd say about a date with your ex, Roger. Not Clay."

Spring sighed. "What do you want me to say, Summer?"

"That you had an exciting, adventurous evening. That you'll never forget a minute of it. Say something romantic and sweet that will make me believe there's still hope for you."

Shaking her head, Spring dropped to sit on the edge of the bed, stretching her bare feet out in front of her on the plush carpet. "Summer, we went to a junior-high-school play and then had dinner at a little Italian restaurant with an odd name that I've already forgotten. Does that sound like the kind of date you just described?"

"No. But then, you were with Clay McEntire. He has a way of making seemingly mundane things extraordinary."

"All right, dammit! My date with Clay was exciting. And adventurous. I'll never forget a single moment of it. Does that make you happy?"

Blinking at her sister's uncharacteristic show of temper, Summer leaned forward slightly. "Was it something I said?"

Spring groaned and hid her face in her hands. "God, I'm sorry. I didn't mean to jump all over you like that. It's just that . . . that . . ." Her voice trailed off.

"Clay's getting to you, right?" Summer tried to sound sympathetic but wasn't particularly successful since her brilliant blue eyes were sparkling with delighted pleasure.

Dropping her hands, Spring straightened her spine. "Okay, so maybe I am a bit . . . infatuated with him," she admitted carefully. "But that's all it is. He's good-looking and interesting and amusing. It's perfectly natural for me to be attracted to him. What woman wouldn't be?"

"Of course," Spring agreed gravely.

"But that doesn't mean that there's anything developing between us. Nothing lasting, I mean. There couldn't be."

"Why not?"

"Why not?" Spring repeated incredulously, jumping to her feet to restlessly pace the room. "Summer, I've only known him for three days. And I'll be leaving California in nine more days. Besides, Clay and I are entirely different. Much too different to even consider a serious relationship."

Summer shook her head vigorously. "Oh, no. That excuse won't wash with me. Remember who you're talking to, Spring. I'm the former party girl married to the ex-spy-turned-businessman, remember? It would be hard to find two people more different than Derek and me, but we love each other so much that we've learned to accept those differences."

"You and Derek aren't as different as you like to imply," Spring argued. "And at least you live in the same state."

"So? People relocate all the time. I did. Besides, logic and geography have nothing at all to do with this. We're talking about human emotions here. The way you and Clay feel about each other."

"But I don't *know* how I feel about Clay. And I certainly don't know what he feels for me."

"Are you kidding? The guy's nuts about you! He's had the look of a man who's been poleaxed ever since you walked into my den last Friday. And since Clay is not a man to hide his emotions, I'm sure he's told you exactly how he feels."

Call it love, he'd said. But she couldn't call it that. She just couldn't.

"He's told me that he's attracted to me," Spring admitted. "He's convinced we're going to have an affair."

"And would that be so awful?" Summer teased.

Spring took a deep breath and glanced at her sister, knowing her feelings were all too clear on her face. "It just might be devastating," she whispered.

Her sister's mischievous smile faded immediately and was replaced by a look of compassion. "Spring—"

"Summer, you're not in here grilling your sister for details about her date tonight, are you?" Derek's voice inquired blandly from the open doorway.

"Why, Derek. Am I the type of person to pry into someone else's personal business?"

"Yes, you are," Derek and Spring replied in smiling, unhesitating unison.

Spring thought again how very much she liked her brother-in-law. Summer tossed her head indignantly and climbed as gracefully as she could from Spring's bed. "I won't stay here and let the two of you insult me," she announced with great dignity. "I'm going to bed."

"Good night, Summer," Spring bade her fondly. "Good night, Derek," she added as he left the room with a conspiratorial wink at her.

Summer glanced back over her shoulder as she limped from the room. "Sleep well, Sis. Try not to worry about anything, okay?"

Spring assured her sister that she would sleep like a log, but she was lying through her teeth. She wouldn't sleep a wink for thinking of Clay. Her body still tingled from the desire that he'd aroused in her, desire such as she'd never known before. What was it that he did to her?

Call it love.

No, she wouldn't call it love. Not that.

DURING THE NEXT TWO DAYS Spring discovered that Clay was a man who carried through with his promises—and threats. It seemed that every time she turned around he was there. On Tuesday night he showed up on the Andersons' doorstep and invited himself to dinner. He stayed three and a half hours. During that time he patted Spring's shoulder five times, hugged her twice, squeezed her hand nine times, kissed her cheek once and kissed her mouth twice briefly and once thoroughly. She counted.

By the time he left, she was on fire. She took a long, cold shower before going to bed, but all that did was give her goose bumps. It did absolutely nothing to dampen her newly awakened libido.

On Wednesday Clay called Summer and offered to take the three of them to dinner that evening. Being the determined matchmaker that she was, Summer cheerfully accepted. Spring tried to act annoyed, but they both knew that the scolding was only a formality. The truth was that Spring couldn't wait to see Clay again, and she and Summer both knew it.

Dressed in cream and a delectable shade of mint green, Clay was at his outrageous best from the moment the evening began. He teased the others until they laughed helplessly, then laughed good-naturedly when they teased him right back. Spring spent much of the evening capturing his wandering hands and returning them firmly to him, her stern looks not very adequately concealing what those daring touches did to her.

She could have gladly strangled him when he introduced her to their waiter—who turned out to be a former student of his—as the woman he would like to have an affair with. Eyeing her vivid blush, the young waiter grinned, congratulated Clay on his excellent taste and provided a bottle of champagne to further the cause.

"You," Spring told Clay through clenched teeth, "are going to die."

"Have an affair with me," he retorted, "and I'll die happy."

Summer and Derek laughed, greatly enjoying the entertainment provided by the other couple.

"Walk me to my car, Spring," Clay ordered some time later after nightcaps in the Andersons' den. "I've got to go."

"I'm sure you can find your way to the driveway," Spring replied blandly, not moving from her chair.

"Aw, c'mon," he whined boyishly. "There's something I want to show you."

"That's exactly what I'm worried about," Spring retorted, much to Summer's and Derek's amusement. They all knew that the "something" he wanted to show her was nothing more than a ploy to get her alone. Still, she stood, with a great show of reluctance, and walked out with him.

It was a dream of a night. Cool, fragrant, inhabited by dancing fog wraiths and twinkling diamond lights spreading out for miles around them. Spring closed her eyes and inhaled, then opened them to survey the glory around her. "Beautiful, isn't it?" she murmured to Clay.

He turned and leaned against his low sports car, catching her forearms to pull her into a loose embrace. "I used to think so."

"You used to?" Almost without thinking about it, she rested her hands on his shoulders, her lower body settling lightly against his. "What happened?"

"I met you." His arms tightened around her. "Now I compare everything I see to your beauty. Nothing else measures up."

It should have sounded trite, corny. It did, of course, she assured herself, but it still made her knees go weak. She tried to sound annoyed, but her voice came out all breathless. "That's dumb. Besides, I'm not beautiful."

He lowered his mouth to within an inch of hers. "Yes, you are," he murmured.

"No, I'm—" She stopped, swallowed, then finally moaned. "Oh, Clay, please kiss me."

"Thank you," he said unexpectedly, then took her lips with the familiar hunger that was more overwhelming each time he kissed her.

Spring slipped her arms around his neck and pressed closer, her mouth opening eagerly under his. His hands were warm and searching over the lightweight sweater she wore, stroking her curves and contours with open palms. A tiny whimper lodged itself in her throat when his fingertips slid between the hem of her sweater and the waistband of her skirt to trace the soft skin there, then moved around and upward to cup one of her small breasts through the fabric of her bra.

"You *are* beautiful, Spring," he muttered against her mouth. "And I want you so much." He rocked her gently against his lower body, against the proof of his wanting. "I need you."

"Clay, I—" She caught her breath when he rolled her hardened nipple between thumb and forefinger, the sensation shooting from her breast to some deep, yearning part of her. "Oh, Clay."

He kissed her again, his tongue surging between her slightly swollen lips to stroke hers, withdrawing, then sliding back in. The sensual imagery made her weak with desire, and she arched against him in an unconscious plea for the ultimate intimacy. His hands fell to her hips, holding her almost painfully against his straining manhood for a moment before moving her a few inches away from him. His voice was raw with his need. "God, Spring. Much more of this and we'll end up making love right here in your sister's driveway."

She groaned in chagrin and dropped her hot face to his shoulder, pulling in a painfully ragged breath.

"What do you do to me, Clay McEntire?" she breathed. "At home I'm so sensible, so firmly in control. With you I'm like a stranger. Impulsive and impetuous and even a little wild. I don't know how you do it."

"Don't you like what I do to you, Spring?" he asked whimsically, his own breathing returning slowly to normal.

"Yes, dammit. But it won't last, Clay. I'll go back to Little Rock next week and I'll be myself again. I'm . . . comfortable with my life there."

He was silent for a long moment, his cheek resting against her hair, which she'd worn straight and loose to her shoulders. Finally he spoke, almost reluctantly. "Is there someone special at home, Spring? Are you involved with anyone?"

"Not anymore."

He digested that, along with her tone. "Tell me about him."

"His name is Roger, and he's an attorney. Very attractive, very pleasant. We dated for almost six months. We had a lot in common, wanted the same things in life. Successful careers, marriage, family. A few months ago we realized that we didn't want those things with each other, so we said goodbye."

"Sounds sad," he said thoughtfully.

"It was, in a way. I cried when our relationship ended, but I think the tears were due more to the end of a pleasant fantasy than to the loss of Roger."

Clay raised his arms to cup her face between his hands, his eyes intense in the artificial light. "I don't ever want to make you cry, Spring. I never want to hurt you."

Was he warning her not to start wanting the same things from him that she'd thought she'd wanted from

Roger? He didn't need to. Spring had known all along that Clay wasn't the type who would be content with someone like her. Perhaps he was intrigued with her now, but it wouldn't last. Clay thrived on excitement, new experiences, adventures. She wasn't the type who could provide such things for him on a regular basis. Nor did she want to try. She just wanted a normal, happy life. She wouldn't mind occasional adventures, some excitement, but she needed sanity, as well. She needed to be loved by a man who needed only her, who would want no woman but her.

And she really wished that man could be Clay.

"I'd better go in," she said at last, a note of weariness creeping into her voice.

"Yes. I'll see you tomorrow."

"Tomorrow?"

He nodded. "There's an open-house reception at Halloran House tomorrow night. Part of our fund-raising drive going on this week. I'd like for you to come with Summer and Derek."

"I'd love to. I'm curious to see this place that you and Summer are so devoted to."

"It's interesting." He dropped a kiss on her lips, a mere ghost of the kisses that had gone before, and set her away from him. "Good night, Spring."

"Good night, Clay."

She slipped into the house, then walked quietly toward the den, deep in thought. Her steps halted abruptly at the doorway. Derek and Summer stood before the room's spectacular glass wall, locked in a passionate embrace. Derek's head was bent protectively over his petite wife as he kissed her with familiar intimacy, her arms clenched around his neck.

Spring turned silently and headed for her room, wondering why she suddenly found herself blinking back tears.

CLAY BENT over the bed, his lips touching soft, cool skin as his hand stroked a headful of crisp black curls. "Hi, beautiful."

Liquid brown eyes smiled into his tender blue-green ones. "Hi."

"How're you feeling?"

"Not so great," Thelma whispered, turning her head restlessly on the flat pillow of her intensive-care bed. "My chest hurts like crazy."

"I'm sorry. Is there anything I can do to help?"

"No, but thanks, anyway. What time is it? I lose track in here."

"It's seven-thirty a.m.," he answered. "Thursday," he added, in case she'd also lost track of the days.

"How'd you get in here? I thought only family was allowed in. Not that I'm complaining. I'm so glad to see someone besides my loving mother." She added a bitter twist to the last two words that wrenched Clay's heart.

"I sweet-talked a nurse," he told her, deliberately maintaining his easy smile. "Told her I was your brother."

Thelma laughed weakly, lifting their clenched hands and eyeing the contrast between her brown and his fair skin. "And she bought it, right? You're slick, man."

"Thanks. I try." He glanced at all the tubes and wires attached to her, trying not to frown. Thelma remained a very sick young woman. The doctors still hesitated to predict whether her recovery would be complete, continuing to worry about permanent lung damage—

the delicate membranes had been so badly scarred by her neglect of her condition. Clay refused even to consider the possibility that Thelma could still die. "I talked to Frank this morning. He said that you're going to Chicago to live with your aunt when you leave the hospital."

Thelma nodded. "That's right. I been begging to go live with Aunt Diane for a long time, but my mother refused to let me. She's finally given in."

"Think you'll be happy in Chicago?"

The shrug she gave was heartbreakingly old for her age. "Who knows? But it couldn't be any worse than here. And Aunt Diane seems to want me with her. First time anyone's wanted me around in a long time."

"That's not quite true, Thelma. I've always wanted you around."

"Yeah, but we both know that you're a bleeding heart. Always have been, always will be."

"You got it," Clay admitted, winking at her.

"Well, you can stop bleeding over me. I've decided to get it together in Chicago. Aunt Diane says if I'll straighten up and really try to do better, she'll see that I get the money to go to college when I finish high school, major in music, like I've always wanted to do. The doctors won't tell me whether I'll be able to sing worth a damn, uh—" she paused, knowing how Clay felt about "his kids" cursing, then continued "—halfway good after this thing with my lungs, but I'm going to do it, one way or another. If I can't sing, I've always got my piano. I'm pretty good, you know."

"I've always been your number one fan, haven't I?"

"Yeah. You have. Thanks. Sorry I keep screwing up."

"Everyone screws up sometimes, Thel. Now you've just got to put the past behind you and try again. You can do it."

She sighed wearily and closed her eyes for a moment, her lashes delicate against youthful cheeks. Then her eyes opened again, and there was a sheen of tears. "I haven't thanked you for saving my life."

"It's okay. You don't have to."

"I really didn't care if I died, you know."

Clay's throat tightened. "I know. But I cared. And Frank and Summer cared. And your Aunt Diane cares. We love you, Thelma, and we're going to save your life and your future even if we have to kick your butt to get you to listen to us."

She chuckled faintly. "All right. I said I'd try." She paused again, and Clay could see that she was tiring. He moved as if to leave, but her hand tightened on his. "Don't go yet. Please. It gets lonely in here."

"All right. I've got a few more minutes before the nurse kicks me out."

"That woman who was with you when you found me . . . who was she?"

Startled, Clay tilted his head. "Her name is Spring Reed. Summer's sister. Do you remember her?"

"I think so. It's real fuzzy, but I sort of remember a pretty lady with blond hair washing my face and talking to me in a nice, friendly voice. I remember how good it felt. I was so hot."

"Spring will be glad to hear that. She's been worried about you. She's another bleeding heart, like Summer and me," he added, using Thelma's own words to tease her.

"Are you in love with her?" Thelma asked unexpectedly, reading something in his voice or his expression as she watched him closely.

He blinked, then grinned rather sheepishly. "Yeah. Yeah, I am."

"Going to marry her?"

"Haven't thought about it. I'm not really the marrying kind, you know."

"Bull."

He raised one eyebrow, questioningly. "I beg your pardon?"

"I said bull. You act crazy, but everyone knows you're just Joe Normal underneath. You'd be happy as a clam with a wife and a bunch of kids and *you* know it. So don't try to con me, McEntire."

"Think so, huh?"

"Know so." Her lashes fell again. "I'm getting sleepy. Sorry."

"That's okay. You need your rest, and it's time for me to get to school. I stopped by here on the way to work, and I'd better go or I'll be late. But I'll be back."

"Promise?"

"Promise. And you'd better write to me when you're in Chicago, or I'll come after you, you hear?"

"Yeah?" She looked inordinately pleased. "Will you write me back?"

"You can count on it." He kissed her cheek, then straightened. "I'll see you tomorrow."

"Okay." She stopped him at the entrance to her glass cubicle. "Clay?"

"Yeah?"

"You're dressed kinda boring today, aren't you?"

He grinned, looking down at his lime-green T-shirt, worn Levi's and white Reeboks. "I dressed in a hurry this morning. I'll try to do better next time."

"You do that. This place is dull enough. Bye, Clay."

He left with his grin still in place, though inside he was praying fervently that the teenager would recover. She deserved a break.

EXHALE. CLAY LOWERED his chin almost to the floor, his forearms straining under his weight. *Inhale.* He pushed himself up so that his body was on a slant, mentally counting, *forty-nine.*

Exhale. He lowered himself again, sweat dripping down his forehead. *Inhale. Fifty.*

With a grunt he abruptly threw himself onto his back, crossing his hands on his bare, sweat-slick chest. He really hated exercising, he thought ruefully. That's why he never did it. Good thing he stayed in shape through his usual frenetic activity.

So why was he trying to turn himself into melting Jell-O with push-ups? Good question. And he knew the answer. He was trying not to think of Spring. He'd been trying not to think of her all day, since his early-morning visit with Thelma. He'd tried not to think about her during his hours at work, during lunch with his friend Frank from Halloran House, during seventy-five sit-ups and fifty push-ups.

It wasn't working. It seemed as if she'd been on his mind since the moment he'd set eyes on her.

Okay, so he was in love with her. He'd known before Thelma had made him admit it that morning; had, in fact, known since he'd seen her in her "funky" outfit

Monday evening. And it was going to hurt when she left next Wednesday. It was going to hurt bad.

He'd never felt quite like this before. The few times he'd flirted with love in the past had usually been pleasant, sometimes passionate, but never permanent. And he'd never particularly regretted that fact. He'd always put his work first. Something told him he wouldn't get over Spring as easily. The same something that told him that his work wouldn't be quite enough when she was hundreds of miles away from him. He almost resented her for that.

Six days. She was flying out of his life in six days. His stomach clenched with dread.

He'd known a lot of emotions in his thirty-four-plus years. Despair, disillusion, hopelessness, rage. Later he'd discovered fulfillment, hope, love and happiness. He'd rarely known fear. But he was scared now. He'd tried so hard to make his life work, to fill the emptiness that had yawned inside him through the lonely, unhappy years of his youth. He lived alone now, but he hadn't consciously been lonely. He was pretty damned sure that he would be lonely in seven days. And in ten, and maybe even in one hundred, and more. Lonely for Spring.

He'd never loved this way before; he couldn't imagine loving like this again. Couldn't imagine himself making love to any woman but Spring. It had never been like this before.

Maybe he should back off a bit. Start preparing himself for being without her. Stop thinking about her all the time, counting the hours until he saw her again. Stop wondering what it would take to make her stay with him in six days.

Grinding a rare curse between clenched teeth, he flipped onto his stomach and flattened his palms on his bedroom carpet. His arm muscles bulged.

Inhale. Exhale. Fifty-one.

Six more days.

Inhale. Exhale. Fifty-two.

6

HALLORAN HOUSE WAS a fascinating place, Spring decided. The twenty-odd residents were young, between the ages of eleven and sixteen, had been in trouble, but not too serious trouble yet, and wore defiant expressions that seemed to refuse intimacy yet pleaded for love all at the same time. Clay informed Spring that because the home, which had been established by a wealthy industrialist who had lost a son to a drug overdose, was funded primarily by donations, several major fund-raising events took place each year. The residents had put on a talent show last fall, which was how Summer had gotten involved. Clay had drafted her to direct the show.

The current effort was an open-house reception for patrons and potential patrons. An informal buffet had been set up in the former ballroom-turned-recreation room, and a presentation was made to outline the home's purpose. Dressed all in white—shirt, coat, vest, pants, shoes and, yes, a white tie—Clay was a highly visible participant in the program. Spring couldn't take her eyes off him, but her fascination with him had little, if anything, to do with his clothing. Instead, she watched the way the light played on the golden highlights in his blond hair, the way his laughter made his eyes sparkle, the flashing dimples that appeared as deep grooves at the side of his mouth when he smiled. It seemed that every time she saw him, he was even more beautiful.

"What do you think of my kids?" he asked Spring at one point as he snatched a moment of semiprivacy with her by crowding her into a corner.

Spring turned her head to look past him. Many of the guests had gone by that time, leaving mostly staff and residents gathered in small clusters in the recreation room. "Some of them look pretty tough," she remarked. "And impressively big for their ages. Do you ever have trouble with them?"

"Sure, sometimes. Fights, threats, whatever. We've learned to deal with it."

"How does Summer deal with it?"

"Very well." Clay's lips quirked upward. "Not that she has that much trouble. The kids think she's really 'hot,' in their vernacular. They tease with her, but they're actually quite respectful to her. Protective, even. And then they have one little extra incentive to be nice to her."

"What's that?"

Leaning against the wall behind him, he caught her hand and laced his fingers through hers. "A couple of months ago we were having some real problems with one of our larger, more troubled kids. He's fifteen, and big. Anyway, Summer directs some drama classes, improv, readings, and so on, because we feel it's good for the kids to express themselves creatively. Most of them like it; some don't. This guy started making trouble during one session, making fun of the smaller kids until he finally had one of them crying. Then he made fun of him for being a crybaby. Summer got mad and told the guy off. He decided to show everyone how bad he could be, so he gave her a shove."

Spring frowned, instantly the protective big sister. "Did he hurt her? Was he punished? He's not still here, is he?"

Clay laughed, his hand tightening reassuringly around hers. "It's okay. The kid made a bit of a mistake. Derek happened to walk into the room just as the guy pushed Summer down."

A slight smile crept across Spring's face. "Oh. That *was* a mistake, wasn't it?" she mused, thinking of her businessman brother-in-law and the toughness she'd sensed in him from the beginning.

"You got it. I'd come into the room right behind Derek, and I thought he was going to tear the kid apart. The kid thought so, too. He got off with nothing more than a deadly soft warning. He's treated Summer like fine porcelain ever since. He was dealt with officially here, of course, but it was Derek's threat that kept him straight from then on."

Spring tilted her head. "I'd be willing to bet that Summer got mad at Derek for interfering."

"Know her well, don't you? She did, as a matter of fact. Said she was perfectly capable of handling the situation herself."

"She probably could have."

"I've no doubt of it. But Derek never apologized to her. He just sat quietly while she chewed him out, then told her in that silky voice of his that he'll do exactly the same thing if the situation ever comes up again. And that he's fully prepared to carry through on his threats if necessary."

"Mr. Macho." Spring sighed, shaking her head. She'd left her hair down that evening and it fell in a silvery blond curtain to curl at her shoulders, where it swayed against her peach silk dress at her movement.

Clay reached out with his free hand to catch a soft strand, rubbing it between his fingers as he murmured, "I suddenly see Derek's point. It's amazing how protective a man can feel about his woman." He met her eyes. "I know how I'd react if I found some guy shoving you to the floor."

She blinked. *Make it a joke*, she told herself in a desperate attempt to lighten a suddenly heavy moment. "My, my. I do believe there's a bit of macho even in you, Clay."

He grinned and allowed her to ease the tension with her teasing. "What can I say? I'm a mere male, after all."

"Pity," she murmured, tugging her hand from his and stepping back. "I believe I'll have some more of that punch."

She sipped her punch slowly, thinking that she was almost sorry she'd backed away from Clay a moment before. Oddly enough, when he'd taken her hand, it had been the first time he'd really touched her all evening. He'd been acting rather strangely since she'd arrived with Summer and Derek earlier. Though he'd carried on in his usual offbeat manner, there'd been something different in his manner toward her. It was almost as if he'd withdrawn from her in some way.

She couldn't help thinking of their conversation the night before. He'd offered to back away from her, but she'd weakly asked him not to. So why was he?

She frowned as a sudden thought occurred to her. What if he'd been put off by her telling him about Roger? In her moment of vulnerability she'd told Clay that she fantasized about marriage and family. Was he afraid that she'd start considering him as potential-husband material, as she'd admitted to doing with Roger? Was he backing off, as he'd said he would, in a subtle attempt to warn her not to get too involved with him? It made sense, but she wasn't sure. After all, he'd just implicitly called her his woman, hadn't he? Or had he?

No one had ever confused her the way Clay did, she thought, her mind growing weary from trying to understand him. And no one had ever made her want so very badly to understand him.

She watched him across the room, clowning around with a group of his kids. He loved them so much. She suspected that love, for him, would be an obsession. What would it be like to be loved that way by him?

She'd like to find out, she thought wistfully.

She swallowed hard and set her punch cup on a table. What was she thinking? What did she hope would happen? Could she even imagine leaving the successful practice she'd built for herself in Little Rock to move to California, where the competition would be so fierce? She loved Arkansas. Unlike her sisters, she was perfectly happy to remain in the state where she'd been born.

She tried to make herself stop thinking along those lines. She was being ridiculous. There was nothing serious between her and Clay. Nor did he appear to want anything more than a temporary alliance between them. He was a confirmed bachelor who dated women her own sister had described as drop-dead beautiful. He probably liked his life just the way it was—one beautiful woman after another, no strings, no messy entanglements. Nothing to offer a woman like her, who wanted . . . who needed so much more.

"Spring, I'd like you to meet Katie," Summer said, appearing suddenly at her sister's side. "She's a real sweetheart. You'll like her."

Fervently grateful for the distraction, Spring obediently followed Summer across the room.

Though he was talking heartily, appearing to be completely involved in his conversation, Clay knew every move Spring made across the room from him. It seemed that he was aware of each breath she took, though they were separated by several yards. It was no use, he decided fatalistically, even as he gave a light-hearted reply to a question that had just been thrown at him. He wasn't going to be able to insulate himself from her, no matter how hard he might try.

And he had tried. All evening he'd attempted to look at her and see just another pretty, interesting woman. Nothing special. Right?

Wrong. She was beautiful, more so each time he saw her. She was fascinating. And he was in love with her.

And she was going to be with him for only six more days.

Okay, so he was going to miss her when she left. Okay, so it would hurt. What was he going to do about it?

Only one thing to do, he decided abruptly. He'd take advantage of every moment of the next six days that he could spend with her. He'd make love to her as soon as he could persuade her, and if that didn't satisfy his appetite for her, he'd make love to her again. And again. And again, until she was as steeped in him as he was in her.

Maybe then she would stay.

IT WAS WITH MIXED FEELINGS that Spring accompanied Summer, Derek and Clay to a party in the home that Connie Anderson shared with Joel Tanner. She wasn't overly excited about attending a party where she knew only five other people, but it *was* another excuse to be with Clay. Summer had even stopped teasing her about seeing so much of Clay, and Derek, in his placid way, seemed to accept Clay's constant presence as inevitable while Spring was around. Spring was beginning to feel like one of a couple. She liked the feeling. She was going to miss it when it ended in five days.

Connie had moved in with Joel a month earlier, in February. They planned to be married in May, when Connie and Derek's parents returned from a leisurely, long-planned cruise, but they saw no need to wait that long to live together. This was Connie's first real party in her new home. It was cheerful, loud, eccentric. Good clean fun, Summer assured her sister.

"It's not Derek's and Joel's kind of thing, either, but they'll have a good time," she added as she helped Spring select a casual outfit consisting of a peach cotton blouse and comfortably full peach-and-cream plaid skirt.

"It's *your* kind of thing, though, isn't it?" Spring asked thoughtfully. "And Clay's."

"Sure, I love parties. So does Clay. He gets to perform."

"Perform?"

Summer only smiled mysteriously. "You'll see."

Yes, Spring thought glumly. She was afraid that she *would* see. She'd see, again, how very different she and Clay were. And, worse, he'd see the same thing. She wondered if any of his beautiful women would be there.

They were. From the moment Clay entered the room, Spring at his side, he was deluged by affectionate welcomes. Women—redheads, blondes, brunettes, all disgustingly beautiful—greeted him with kisses and hugs, teasing him about things that Spring didn't know about, illustrating so clearly how far apart their lives were. The women were dressed casually, for the most part, but with daring style that made Spring feel very provincial and unsophisticated next to them.

The music was loud, classic rock and roll mostly. Spring liked rock and roll, but it did make conversation rather difficult. She smiled a lot.

When Bob Seger's recorded voice burst out with "Old Time Rock 'n Roll," everyone laughed and tried to talk Clay into stripping down to his shirt and briefs and doing the lip-sync routine that Tom Cruise had made famous in the movie *Risky Business*. Clay declined with a laugh, but Spring got the impression that he wouldn't always have turned down the challenge. It seemed that he had done that particular routine at several other parties. He only laughed and shrugged when she turned a questioning glance on him.

Spring managed to have a good time at the party, despite her initial feeling that she was terribly out of place, until a striking brunette joined the party halfway through the evening. She was dressed in Chinese red, red silk blouse and matching slacks that looked as if she'd been poured into them, and she was on the arm of an attractive auburn-haired man everyone called Ace. Spring sensed immediately that Connie and Summer hadn't known the woman would be there as Ace's date. She caught the quick, startled glances the former roommates exchanged before greeting the woman with somewhat stilted politeness.

Clay hadn't known the woman would be at the party, either, Spring realized a few moments later. She just happened to be watching his face when he caught sight of the brunette. His eyes narrowed, and a muscle twitched in his jaw. His expression was hard to read, but Spring thought she detected chagrin. Then he glanced at her, caught her watching him and smiled, his face revealing nothing of his thoughts.

Who was she and what was she, or what had she been, to Clay? Spring asked herself the question with a fierce surge of jealousy that left her dismayed and wary. She couldn't allow herself to go on this way, she tried to tell herself sternly. She must *not* fall in love with Clay McEntire!

It was all she could do not to demand an explanation from Clay when he placed his arm lightly around her shoulders and asked if she wanted a drink from the bar. "A club soda sounds nice," she said, then wondered if she should have asked for something stronger. Though she rarely drank, this night might be a good time for it.

The woman cornered them before he could even reply. It was as if she'd homed in on Clay the moment she entered the room and had barely paused on her way to him. "Hello, Clay."

"Hello, Jessica," he returned, a hint of resignation in his voice. His arm tightened around Spring's shoulders, just a little, as if the movement had been nothing more than reflex.

"Surprised to see me here?"

"Yes, I am a bit. I thought you'd left San Francisco."

She nodded, her rather slanted green eyes sparkling with feminine amusement, deep red mouth quirked into a slightly feline smile. "I did. I'm back."

"So I see."

"I wasn't at all surprised to see you. I knew you'd be at this party since you used to take me to all of Connie and Summer's parties."

"How clever of you." He managed to sound amazed and sarcastic all at once.

Her long lashes flicking in apparent annoyance, she eyed him slowly, her gaze lingering intimately on the tight black pants below his blousy, full-sleeved white shirt. Spring felt her hands curling into claws even as the woman drawled, "What is this, your Errol Flynn look? Love those knee-high boots. Quite dashing."

"Thanks." As if he'd just remembered his manners, Clay tightened his arm around Spring again and glanced down at her with a vaguely apologetic smile. "Sorry, sweetheart. This is Jessica Dixon, an old friend. Jess, meet Spring Reed, Summer's sister."

Jessica hadn't liked being called an "old" friend any more than Spring had liked his familiar shortening of the other woman's name. "It's very nice to meet you, Spring," she said in a voice that said it wasn't really all that nice. She'd barely looked Spring's way before she turned back to Clay. "Clay, darling, you haven't even kissed me hello. Surely that's not too much to expect after all we've been to each other."

That did it. Spring decided she didn't need to stand around and let the woman rub her face in the fact that Jessica and Clay had been lovers. "Clay, I think Joel is signaling for you," she said firmly. "Don't you think we should go see what he wants?"

"Yes, Spring, I think we should do just that," he replied gravely, his eyes and voice ripe with amusement. "See you later, Jess."

They were all the way across the room—nowhere near Joel and making no pretense to find him—before Spring spoke to Clay. "Could I ask just one question?"

Warily he nodded. "Of course."

"Was that the same woman you were with the night you met Summer?"

He grinned. "No."

She lifted an imperious eyebrow behind her glasses, trying to sound regal and condescending. "You have a thing for bitchy brunettes?" she asked distastefully.

"I suppose I did at one time," he answered thoughtfully, looking rather surprised at his own answer. Then he winked at her. "Guess I knew they were safe enough to hang around with until I found a particularly sweet blond."

She tossed her head. "Just don't feed me any lines right now, will you, Clay?"

Unable to resist, he hugged her. "Why, Spring Reed, I do believe you're jealous."

She glared at him. "Yes, dammit, I am. And I know full well that it's stupid and illogical and totally unjustified, so just don't start with me, McEntire, or I'll . . . I'll . . . I'll walk out of here and leave you to that barracuda!"

"Oh, please, not that!" he murmured, laughing softly. On his face was a look of such wholly masculine satisfaction that Spring wanted to hit him. She really did.

"I want a drink," she told him flatly. "And I *don't* want club soda."

"Anything you desire, sweetheart," he answered her with mock subservience. "If you're tipsy, it will be all the easier to seduce you later."

She refused to respond to that in any way.

She wasn't tipsy, but he came close to seducing her, anyway. They had left the party not long after the encounter with Jessica. Clay claimed that he had a headache. The other guests actually believed him; it seemed that he'd been exceptionally well behaved that evening. Summer went so far as to call him "dull." Spring knew good and well that the headache was nothing more than a fabrication, but when he innocuously asked if he could stop by his place for an aspirin before taking her back to Sausalito, she told him she didn't mind.

"I can't believe you're stopping this now," Clay complained later in a ragged voice, looming over her on the deep terra-cotta-colored sofa. "We were doing so well."

About half an hour had passed since they'd entered Clay's house. Spring's blouse was open to the waist, her hair completely free of the pins that had once held it, and she was panting and flushed with passion. Clay wasn't in any better condition, his shirt open rakishly to the button of his now indecently tight pants, his hair rumpled boyishly around his face, his eyes unnaturally bright.

She inhaled deeply, tugged her blouse across her straining, well-kissed breasts and shook her head against the sofa cushion. "You promised you'd stop whenever I asked you to," she reminded him huskily.

"Yes, I know. But I kinda wish you'd asked a bit sooner, if you just had to ask." He sighed, running a hand through his hair as he reluctantly sat up.

She chewed guiltily on her lower lip. "I'm sorry. I didn't mean to—It's just that, well, I got a little carried away."

He pulled her into his arms, nuzzling his cheek against hers. "You liked what we were doing, didn't you, Spring?"

She almost moaned at the renewal of feelings she'd just barely gotten under control. "You must know that I did."

"So why are we stopping? I want you, Spring, and I think you want me. You do, don't you?"

Buttoning her blouse, she glanced upward through lowered lashes. "Yes. I want you. But I can't make love with you tonight. The timing's all wrong."

He looked puzzled. "Why?"

Struggling to explain, even to understand herself, she twisted her hands in the lap of her wrinkled plaid skirt. "It's because of that woman."

He didn't have to ask which woman. "Spring, whatever was between Jessica and me was over a long time ago."

"I'm sure that's true. But the point is that I was jealous of her tonight. And I'm afraid that if I made love with you now, it would be because I was competing with her in some way. That's not what I want. I want to be sure I know what I'm doing, and why I'm doing it, before I make such an important decision. I don't take things like this lightly, Clay."

He dropped his forehead to rest it against hers. "Darling Spring, I love everything about you, I really do, but that convoluted mind of yours is driving me insane."

He loved everything about her? She savored the words for a moment. They were a bit like saying he loved her, weren't they? But still not enough. She was so close to loving him. She wouldn't be able to stop herself if they made love now. Maybe it was already too late, but surely she had to try. She had only five more days with him.

BY SATURDAY AFTERNOON Spring knew she'd made a mistake. Hours had passed since she'd last seen or heard from Clay and still her body throbbed with frustration. She wanted him in a way that was all new to her. She'd been stupid to stop him when he'd been making such beautiful love to her, she decided morosely. She wouldn't blame him if he wrote her off as neurotic and stayed completely away from her for the next four days. But how she hoped that he wouldn't!

She and Summer spent the morning roaming through some of the tiny shops of artsy-craftsy novelties for which Sausalito was famous. They examined paintings, pottery, sculpture, handcrafted clothing and accessories . . . and all the time Spring wondered where Clay was, what he was doing. Was he thinking of her? She even wondered irrationally if he was with Jessica.

Stupid, stupid, stupid, she berated herself furiously, staring at a romantic painting of a lovely Victorian home surrounded by vivid flowers. The painting was stylish, beautiful and so very San Francisco. The colors would look wonderful in her apartment, but she couldn't bring herself to purchase it. It would remind her too much of Clay. Something told her she would think of him enough without having such poignant reminders hanging on her wall. *You have to stop this, Spring Reed. You have to stop this . . . this—*

"Moping," Summer said from behind her.

Spring jumped and jerked her head toward her sister. "What?"

"I said, what's with all the moping? You've been off in another world all day. And it doesn't look like such a pleasant world, from the expression on your face. What's wrong, Spring?"

"Nothing. I was just admiring this painting. Lovely, isn't it?"

Summer allowed herself to be distracted, though not without a long, searching look at her sister's face.

Clay called later that afternoon. "I think it's time I introduced you to my cooking," he informed Spring with a wicked chuckle.

"I'm not sure I'm up to this," Spring bantered, though her knuckles were white around the plastic receiver as she gripped it in sheer relief. He hadn't given up. "Are Summer and Derek invited to this culinary experiment?'

"Not this time, sweetheart. This time it's just you and me. No sister, no brother-in-law and no ex-girlfriends. How does that sound?"

She knew what he was asking. And it had very little to do with dinner. "That sounds very nice," she answered him, wondering if he could hear the whispery thread of a voice that came from her throat.

He did. "Good," he said, and his own voice had deepened. "I'll pick you up at seven. Dress sexy." With that he hung up.

Spring stood holding the receiver to her chest, staring into space, until Summer walked into the room and politely inquired if Spring was having an out-of-body experience.

It took her over an hour to get ready for her date. Though she berated herself the entire time for being silly, she was dithered over her selection of clothing. After all, she reasoned nervously, it wasn't as if her date were going to show up in an average suit and tie. Who knew what Clay would choose to wear? Not that she could compete with his flashy style, but she would like him to admire the way she dressed. She settled finally on a slinky jacquard silk dress in a pale mint green. Showing tantalizing hints of cleavage and leg when she moved, the surplice wrap dress was fastened with a wide matching belt that emphasized her small waist.

The belt was the only thing holding the garment together. She'd bought the dress on impulse on that first shopping excursion with Summer. She wondered now if, even then, she'd had Clay in mind when she purchased the sexy garment.

She left her hair loose, skillfully applied pastel makeup and clipped on pearl earrings. She was ready. And her hands were trembling so hard she had to clench them in front of her to try to keep them steady. She'd heard the doorbell a few minutes earlier. She knew that Clay was waiting for her.

"You look beautiful, Spring," Derek told her sincerely when she finally came out of her room.

She gave him a grateful smile.

Summer opened her mouth to say something, noticed the expression on her older sister's face and changed her teasing to a quick compliment.

Clay took one look at her, pulled her into his arms and kissed her, deeply and passionately. She wouldn't have minded at all if her sister and brother-in-law hadn't been standing beside them.

"Clay!" she said, gasping, when he finally released her.

"God, you're beautiful," he told her with a grin, then turned to Summer. "I'm so glad you and Derek are staying home tonight."

Summer giggled. "Thanks a lot, friend. Maybe I should come along to chaperone this date."

"You'll never make it out of the house alive, pilgrim," Clay returned in his best John Wayne voice—mitigated somewhat by the unlined pink blazer and matching slacks he wore with a black-and-pink patterned shirt. Spring couldn't picture John Wayne ever wearing pink.

"You have to be the most uninhibited person I've ever met," she told him on the way to his house, thinking of that kiss in front of her sister and brother-in-law.

Clay chuckled. "I have to admit I'm not particularly dismayed by an audience," he agreed.

She thought of the things she'd learned about his childhood. "Is that why you dress so funny?" she asked curiously. "For attention?"

"Who dresses funny?" he demanded with mock indignation.

He obviously had no intention of allowing the conversation to get too serious, so Spring followed his lead and began to tease him about the unusual outfits he'd worn since she'd arrived.

They'd barely stepped into his house before Clay had her in his arms again. "You're so beautiful tonight," he murmured between brief, nipping kisses, his hands gliding over her silk dress. "I love this dress. Why don't you take it off?"

Her momentary attack of nerves disappeared in her sputter of laughter. "Clay! I thought you were going to serve dinner."

"I am," he assured her, removing her smudged glasses and slipping them into the breast pocket of his jacket. He brushed back a strand of her hair, tucking it behind her ear. "It'll be about an hour before it's ready."

She frowned suspiciously at him. "Then why am I here so early?"

He brushed his lips against her cheek, then dropped his head to nibble at her neck while he toyed with her belt. "For appetizers."

She was going weak and there wasn't a thing she could do about it but close her eyes and cling to him as his warm breath teased her ear. "I suppose . . . you consider this an appetizer?" she asked, her voice reedy.

"Mmm." His tongue darted out to taste the soft spot just below her ear, making her shiver with helpless pleasure. "I want you, Spring. It seems like I've been wanting you all my life."

She'd never had much willpower where this man was concerned. What little she'd started out with finally slipped away, unmissed, as her arms went around his neck. "I want you, Clay. I guess I have ever since the first time you kissed me," she confessed huskily. "I couldn't bear to leave California without ever knowing what it was like to have you make love to me. Please love me now."

Something she'd said made him go rigid, almost as if in pain, and she wondered if she'd spoiled the moment. But then he lowered his head and covered her mouth with his and she knew that everything would be all right. More than all right. Every feminine instinct within her told her that making love with Clay would be the most beautiful experience of her life, a memory to treasure for as long as she drew breath. The thought brought a frisson of fear, even as she trembled with excited anticipation. She suspected that nothing in the future would ever compare to Clay's lovemaking.

Clay released her mouth only to sweep her into his arms, holding her high against his chest. She clung trustingly to him as he moved toward his bedroom with long, confident strides. Spring was embarking on a fantastic adventure, and for the first time in her cautious, conservative life she didn't care about consequences or repercussions.

Say yes to free gifts worth over $20.00

Say YES to a rendezvous with romance, and you'll get 4 classic love stories—FREE! You'll get an elegant bronze letter opener—FREE! And you'll get a delightful surprise—FREE! These gifts carry a total value of over $20.00—but you can have them without spending even a penny!

MONEY-SAVING HOME DELIVERY!

Say YES to Harlequin's Home Reader Service® and you'll enjoy the convenience of previewing 4 brand-new books every month, delivered right to your home before they appear in stores. Each book is yours for only $2.24—26¢ less than the retail price, and there is no extra charge for postage and handling.

SPECIAL EXTRAS—FREE!

You'll get our newsletter, *heart to heart*, packed with news of your favorite authors and upcoming books—FREE! You'll also get additional free gifts from time to time as a token of our appreciation for being a home subscriber.

Say yes to a Harlequin love affair. Complete, detach and mail your Free Offer Card today!

FREE—bronze-and-rosewood letter opener

As a bonus for saying YES to romance, we'll give you this beautiful letter opener as a GIFT! Elegant, with a lovely, supple blade, this bronze letter opener has a dainty rosewood handle. It will make your correspondence a romantic experience! This is FREE as our gift of love.

HARLEQUIN HOME READER SERVICE®

FREE OFFER CARD

4 FREE BOOKS

FREE DELIVERY

Place YES
sticker here

FREE LETTER OPENER

FREE SURPRISE

Please send me 4 Harlequin Temptation® novels, free, along with my free letter opener and surprise gifts as explained on the opposite page.

142 CIH MDPJ

Name _____
(PLEASE PRINT)

Address _____ Apt _____

City _____

State _____ Zip _____

Offer limited to one per household and not valid for present subscribers. Prices subject to change.

PRINTED IN U.S.A.

RUSH! FREE GIFTS DEPT.

BUSINESS REPLY CARD

First Class   Permit No. 717   Buffalo, NY

Postage will be paid by addressee

Harlequin Reader Service ®
901 Fuhrmann Blvd.,
P.O. Box 1867
Buffalo, NY 14240-9952

NO POSTAGE
NECESSARY
IF MAILED
IN THE
UNITED STATES

7

CLAY SET HER on her feet beside his bed, gently, as if she were tiny and frail and, oh, so delicate, rather than tall and firm and healthy. He took her face between his hands—his trembling hands, she noted in wonder—and kissed her with such tender beauty that she almost cried. His abrupt change from passion to sweetness made her head spin. She would never know what to expect from him, nor would she want him to be more predictable. He was Clay, and just by being Clay, he made her weak with wanting him.

Her mouth was moist and soft under his, her lips parting in mute invitation. Clay moaned and touched the tip of his tongue to hers, savoring the taste of her. Had any woman ever felt as good? He couldn't remember. He knew no woman had ever made him shudder. He shuddered when Spring's hands parted his blazer to stroke his chest through his thin cotton shirt. If her touch could do this to him through fabric, how would he react to her hands on his bare skin? He couldn't wait to find out, and yet—

"I think I'm nervous," he murmured, his lips quirking into an almost sheepish smile against hers.

Her hands curled at his shoulders as she leaned back fractionally to look up at him in surprise, her violet eyes luminous in the glow of a bedside lamp. "I can't imagine you ever being nervous about anything," she told him. "You always seem so sure of yourself."

"Not with you." He moved his lips to her cheek, then to her temple. "I'm a basket case right now."

"Why?" Her question was only a whisper as she tilted her face to encourage his ministrations, her eyelids fluttering heavily.

"Because I want to make everything perfect for you. I want to be the perfect lover, say all the right things, touch you in all the right ways. I want to make you forget any other man you've ever known, satisfy you so well that no other man will ever compare to me. I'm not usually a possessive man, but you make me want to possess you, body and soul, heart and mind."

"Clay. . ." She squirmed a little in his arms, as if unsure of how to interpret his low-voiced words, how to respond.

Suddenly uncomfortable himself with the intensity of the moment, he spared her the necessity of response by capturing her lips, the kiss deep and consuming. Still lost in the kiss, he tumbled with her to the bed, reaching for the buckle of her wide belt as they fell. The belt fell away and the dress opened, giving him access to the skin bared by her lacy bra and panty hose. He touched the upper curve of her small breasts, then the silky slope of her flat stomach, fingertips sliding beneath the waistband of her panty hose to tease the quivering area just below her navel. He wanted to reach lower, but he restrained himself, determined to draw their lovemaking out as long as possible.

Her hands tugged at his clothing, making him wonder just how long his noble willpower would last. He shrugged out of his jacket, tossing it to the floor, then tugged his shirt from his slacks. With her eager assistance he freed both of them from everything but his narrow black briefs and her satin-and-lace panties.

"So beautiful. You're so very beautiful." Clay's breath was hot on one of her breasts, his hands restlessly stroking every inch of her that he could reach.

Spring arched into his avid mouth, her fingers deep in his golden hair to hold him closer. His muttered words pleased her. He found her beautiful. Rationally she knew she was pretty, at best. Yet Clay made her feel beautiful. She moaned as he drew the straining, hardened tip of her breast deep into his mouth. Had he really been worried that he wouldn't satisfy her? How silly. Couldn't he tell that he affected her as no man ever had before?

She remembered another time when he had kissed her and she had sensed uncertainty in him. Just as she was attracted to his usual cocky self-confidence, she was fascinated by those glimpses of his vulnerabilities.

Call it love, he'd told her. And though she had fought it, she was beginning to believe that he'd chosen the right word.

Clay lifted his head for a moment to look tenderly down into her passion-flushed face. "Are you protected, sweetheart? If not, I can—"

"No, it's okay. I'm protected," she whispered, touched by his concern. Though there had been no one else since her breakup with Roger, she'd continued to take her birth-control pills, primarily from force of habit. She was glad now that she had.

Smiling his pleasure, Clay continued to caress her breasts with lips and tongue and teeth as his hand stroked downward, moving with tantalizing leisure toward the satin-and-lace triangle that was her only covering. Once there he taunted her further, his fingertips gliding over the fabric so lightly that she wondered if she'd imagined his touch. Gasping, she arched her hips upward, her thighs parting involuntarily as she silently begged him to deepen the caress. Still he teased her with butterfly touches and hot, biting kisses until she cried out and reached for him, pulling him on top of her.

Laughing throatily, he hugged her hard, burying his face in her hair. She locked her arms around his neck, pressing upward so that she could feel every inch of his damp, warm skin next to hers: her breasts flattening against his chest with its light covering of hair; her long, slender legs twining with his solid, rough ones; his heart pounding against her; his breath raw and ragged in her ear. The signs of his arousal heightened her own, and she whispered his name, telling him how badly she wanted him.

Still he tormented her, thrusting against her, hard and virile and throbbingly aroused. Only the fabric of their underwear kept him from entering her. Her head tossed on the pillow. "Please, Clay, please," she moaned, clutching at his waist.

"I will, sweetheart," he promised her, sliding up and down against her to create a sensual friction that soon had her panting and bucking wildly.

"Clay, *please!*" Was this really her, this mindless creature begging for completion? She'd never lost control like this, never wanted like this. Never ached like this. Was he deliberately trying to drive her out of her mind? "Damn you, Clay," she muttered when he thrust against her again in frustrating simulation of that ultimate intimacy.

Using all her strength, she shoved at his shoulders, rolling him to his side. And then she attacked him, her mouth and hands all over his body as she made him ache for her the same way he'd made her ache for him.

She nibbled and sucked at the taut cords of his neck, then licked swirling patterns in the golden hair around his flat brown nipples, finally moving downward to draw long, low groans from him with her bold caresses. He didn't attempt to stop her, seemed incapable of making the effort, even when she jerked his black briefs away to bare him to more intimacies.

No, this couldn't be Spring Reed, this sexy, insatiable, uninhibited woman exploring Clay's body so wantonly. Taking such unholy pleasure in the soft, guttural cry torn from his throat when her lips and tongue stroked him. "Spring! Ah, God, Spring, *yes!*"

And then he was over her and all barriers were gone and he was plunging inside her to a level so deeply buried within her that she hadn't even known it existed. Moving feverishly, he carried her with him on a mind-shattering journey to a place she'd never been before, never imagined. And he took her there so fast and so hard that, in all the mental replays that would come afterward, she'd never exactly remember the details—only the explosive, climactic conclusion.

"Clay!" His name began as a scream but left her lips a mere whisper as she shuddered again and again beneath the shock waves that followed.

"Spring! Ah, love." And he, too, trembled in the aftermath of a climax so powerful, so unique, that it shocked them both.

He didn't let go of her, only rolled to his side to relieve her of his weight. He pulled her close to him, his arms around her as he snuggled against her back. Their position allowed him to soothingly stroke her breasts and stomach as he pressed his lips to the back of her neck. She closed her eyes and rested, her heart rate slowing, her breathing returning to normal. Even after their incredible lovemaking she gloried in the feel of him. The damp softness against the back of her thigh was satisfying evidence that Clay, too, had found pleasure with her, as if she needed proof.

They lay quiet and still for a long time, satisfied to be together. After a while a deeply contented sigh left her lips, causing Clay to stir and chuckle behind her. He nuzzled into the curve of her shoulder. "Are you sorry?"

"About what? Making love with you?"

"Yes."

She nestled back against him, pulling his arms more tightly around her. "No. I'm not sorry."

"I'm glad. So very glad."

Spring smiled ruefully. "I wasn't going to let this happen, you know. I told myself right from the beginning that I wasn't going to sleep with you."

"You haven't slept with me. You've made love with me, but you haven't slept with me."

She sighed again. "You know what I mean."

"Yes, sweetheart, I know what you mean. And I'm glad you changed your mind."

"I couldn't resist you," she answered, dramatically mournful. "Your fatal charm got to me."

He laughed softly. "Is that what did it?"

"Either that or your fish tie. I'm not sure which one."

"I can see where that would be a hard choice," he agreed solemnly, and then bit her on the back of the neck, making her laughingly chastise him. He lay still for another moment, then asked hesitantly, "I don't suppose I could talk you into staying the night?"

She chewed her lip. "No. I'm sorry, Clay, I can't. I wouldn't feel comfortable with that at all."

"It's okay. I understand. But, God, I'd love to wake up with you in my arms. Spring, I—"

And then he swallowed whatever he had intended to say and kissed her nape, his hand caressing one of her breasts as he did so. Her eyes opened in surprise when her body began to respond to his lazy fondling. Surely he couldn't expect her to . . . ?

But he was still soft against her thigh, and she relaxed, her eyelids closing again. Her nipples were hard and swollen when finally his talented fingers left them to drift downward. "Clay?" she whispered uncertainly, squirming a little when his fingertips slipped into blond curls to trace damp folds.

"Shh, Spring. Just let me love you," he murmured, his cheek against hers as he deepened the caress, stroking over and inside her, slowly increasing the pressure until her breath was catching in tiny sobs of pleasure. "That's it, sweetheart," he encouraged her. "Let me make you feel good."

And he did make her feel good, his fingers taking her just to the edge of fulfillment. By then he was no longer soft but as fully aroused as she. Spring cried out in pleasure when he lifted her leg over his and entered her, his fingers never leaving that damp nest of curls. Then cried out again as she was overcome by spasms of ecstasy so intense that she wanted them never to stop, to go on for an eternity. An eternity with Clay.

She hadn't known she was crying until he rolled her onto her back and leaned over her, gently wiping the tears from her cheek. "I hope these are tears of pleasure," he murmured.

"Yes," she whispered, lifting a trembling hand to lightly stroke her thumb below one of his beautiful eyes. "Are these?"

"Oh, yes." The words held a note of awe, as if he, too, were having trouble believing what had taken place between them, not once but twice. And then he pulled her onto his chest and wrapped her close, and the gesture was so lovingly protective that she almost cried again.

Swallowing hard, she snuggled into the hollow of his shoulder and wondered almost dispassionately what the future held for her. Pain, most certainly, when her time with Clay ended. He'd said nothing about making their relationship permanent, had spoken no words of love. He'd told her only that he wanted her, and desire alone was not enough. Yet the future would also hold such beautiful memories. How could she regret what they'd done? She could only be profoundly grateful that she'd known such joy at least once in her life. She would never have believed that anything could have been so wonderful, had she not experienced it herself.

He must have felt her smile against his skin. "What are you thinking?"

She chuckled. "I was remembering the night I met you. I tried then to imagine what you must be like in bed."

"Did you?" He sounded delighted. "Why, Spring, I'm shocked."

"You mean you didn't wonder the same thing about me?" She tried to sound insulted.

She could hear his grin in his answer. "Of course not. And if you believe that, there's this bridge a few miles from here that I'd like to sell you."

He paused for a moment, then asked curiously, "So what did you think I'd be like in bed?"

"Imaginative, sensitive, considerate, and downright good," she replied humorously, recalling her exact thoughts.

"Mmm. And how *was* I?"

"Feeling insecure, Clay?"

"Come on Spring, I can't stand it! What's your opinion?"

Propping herself on her elbow, she relented and smiled down at him. "That you're imaginative, sensitive, considerate, and downright good."

His smile seemed to light the shadowy corners of the room. "Thank you."

"Believe me, it was entirely my pleasure," she answered with heartfelt fervency.

Then she frowned, suddenly overcome by feminine curiosity. "Well?"

He feigned innocence. "Well, what?"

"How was I?"

"Honestly, Spring, postmortems are so tacky," he drawled, then choked dramatically when her hand enclosed his throat. "Okay, okay, I'll tell."

She released his windpipe and smiled sweetly. "Well? Was I what you expected?"

"No."

"No?" Dismayed, she repeated his answer questioningly.

Laughing at her expression, he shook his head. "No. I thought you would be prim and proper and just a bit inhibited. Not that I wasn't looking forward to it, anyway, you understand. But had I known how passionate and responsive you really are, I'd have thrown you over my shoulder and hauled you into my bed that first night."

She shook her head. "It's showing again."

Lifting an eyebrow, he glanced downward along his long, perspiration-sheened body. "I beg your pardon?"

She just managed not to laugh. "I mean, that streak of macho in you is showing again."

"Oh, that."

"Idiot." The word came out an endearment. She toyed with the sparse hair on his chest for a while, then peeked through her lashes at his contented face. "Speaking of food . . ."

"Were we?"

"Yes. Don't you think dinner should be ready by now?"

He made a production of checking the time on his watch. "Why, yes, I do believe it is. Are you hungry, sweet Spring?"

"As a matter of fact, I am. I seem to have worked up quite an appetite since we arrived."

He climbed out of the bed and stood unselfconsciously nude, looking down at her. She almost grabbed him and pulled him back into bed, but she decided that she wouldn't survive another session of lovemaking without sustenance. She laughed when he offered her his robe. The heavy brocade garment was straight out of a Noel Coward movie—velvet lapels, cuffs, one deep pocket. It trailed a foot behind her when she walked. She pushed the voluminous sleeves up on her forearms and scowled at him when he tied himself into a thigh-length white terry robe. "Maybe we should trade."

"I kind of like you in that one," he returned teasingly. "It's interesting for *you* to be the one dressed funny for a change."

"So you admit that you dress funny!"

He only laughed.

She frowned at him, struck by a sudden unpleasant thought. "This robe wasn't a present from a woman, was it?"

"Well, yes, it was," he answered thoughtfully.

She immediately began to untie it. His hand covered hers on the sash. "Summer gave it to me for a Christmas present. She said it reminded her of me, for some strange reason."

She had the grace to look sheepish. "Oh. I was being unreasonably jealous again, wasn't I?"

"Yes, you were." He turned to walk out of the room, then tossed her a cheeky grin. "*This* is the robe that was a present from an old girlfriend," he informed her, straightening his white terry lapels as he walked out.

The shoe she threw after him missed him by mere inches.

The gourmet dinner Clay had offered turned out to be a deli picnic, neatly packed into a basket on the kitchen counter.

"I thought you said you were cooking," Spring accused him, watching him unpack the tempting delicacies onto a round oak kitchen table.

"I said I was going to introduce you to my cooking," he corrected her imperturbably. "This is the way I cook."

"You're a fraud and a scoundrel, Clay McEntire, and I—" She stopped short, then continued lightly, "I really should be angry with you, but I'm just too hungry."

She avoided his eyes as she took her seat across the table from him.

She'd almost told him that she loved him. She wasn't sure exactly when she'd realized it, but she knew now,

And, for the life of her, she didn't know what she was going to do about it.

He'd almost told her he loved her while they were in bed. It would have been so natural, so easy. And so true. God, how he'd wanted to tell her. But he couldn't. He didn't think she wanted to hear it. And, for the life of him, he didn't know what he'd have said afterward.

Clay kept his gaze on the plate in front of him and concentrated on his dinner. They were both unusually quiet while they ate.

HOLDING HER PRESSED AGAINST Summer's front door, Clay kissed Spring good-night. He could never get enough of the taste of her, he decided, lingering over the embrace. No matter how many times he had her, he would never stop wanting her. "It's very late. Are you tired?" he murmured, stroking the faintest of violet shadows under her eyes. She'd kept her glasses in her purse on the way home, anticipating his kiss, he hoped.

"Mmm. Pleasantly so." She tilted her head back against his arm to smile at him in a way that brought an almost painful lump to his throat. He could almost imagine that she loved him when she smiled at him that way. It hurt, he discovered.

"I suppose I should let you go in." He made no attempt to mask his reluctance to release her.

"I suppose so." She sounded no more enthused about the idea.

"I've got things to do tomorrow at Halloran House, so I may not see you."

She bit her lip in visible dismay, then made an effort to sound only politely interested. "That's okay."

"I'll call you."

"Please do."

He kissed her again. "Tonight was . . ." He paused, laughed briefly and shook his shaggy blond head. "I don't know what tonight was. I have nothing to compare it to. Let's just say that it was the most exciting, miraculous, wonderful night of my life."

"Mine, too. I'll never forget it, Clay." She kissed his chin. "You've given me a lovely memory to take home with me."

He felt as if a fist had just slammed into his gut. He just managed not to grunt with the pain. How could she talk about leaving him after all they'd shared so recently? She couldn't, he decided, not if she loved him. He was suddenly glad that he hadn't voiced his own feelings. He'd dealt with enough rejection in his life. He didn't need to go looking for it.

"Yeah, well . . ." He inhaled deeply and forced himself to step back from her. "I'll call you tomorrow."

He drove home, walked straight to the rarely touched bar and poured himself a drink, hoping it would help him forget that the woman he loved was leaving him in four days.

Spring climbed wearily into her bed, grateful that her sister hadn't waited up for her this time, buried her face in her pillow and fell asleep. She woke the next morning with traces of tears on her cheeks, though she couldn't remember crying in her sleep.

"ARE YOU GOING TO TELL ME about it or not?" Summer demanded, her voice carrying clearly. "Did you go to bed with Clay?"

"Summer!" Spring flushed and hastily looked up and down the supermarket produce aisle, hoping that no one had overheard her outspoken sister. "Honestly."

Summer sighed but lowered her voice. "Well? Want to explain that dreamy look that's been in your eyes all day?"

"You know that this is absolutely none of your business."

"Yes, I know."

"And that it's rude and insensitive for you to even ask."

"I know that, too." Summer waited expectantly, her hand hovering over the kiwifruit.

Spring exhaled in a gust of exasperation and shook her head. The truth was, she found herself *wanting* to talk about Clay, about her feelings for him. She thought it just might help her clarify those feelings for herself if she could discuss them with someone loving and sympathetic. Like her sister. "All right, we'll talk about it," she said. "But not in a supermarket! Over lunch."

"Fine."

"So let's talk about you and Clay," Summer demanded as soon as they'd seated themselves at the cozy kitchen table for lunch. Derek was playing golf that afternoon with Joel, giving the sisters a chance to spend time with each other. "Something's going on, I can tell."

With little evidence of success Spring fought the wave of color that flooded her fair cheeks. "Well, we, uh—"

Summer nodded solemnly. "And?"

"And . . . it was, um—"

"I see. So now what?"

"I wish I knew." Spring sighed, shaking her head.

"This is such an enlightening conversation." Summer grinned as she absently stabbed at her fruit salad. "Are you in love with Clay?"

"I strongly suspect that I am."

"Want to try saying that with a smile?"

"I don't think I can. And stop looking so happy, Summer! This is dreadful!"

"Spring, if you're in love with Clay, which you are, and he's in love with you, which I'm sure he is, there's nothing dreadful about it! People in love find ways to work out the obstacles and be together. Derek and I did, Joel and Connie did, and you and Clay will. Be happy, Sis. Falling in love is wonderful, especially when it's the happily-ever-after kind. Believe me, I'm speaking from experience."

"I hope you're right." Spring pushed aside her barely touched plate, knowing how much longing must be written on her face. "I don't know if this is the happily-ever-after kind, but I do know it's permanent. It's not something that's going to go away when I get home."

"Good. Now you know why your other relationships never lasted. You weren't in love."

"No, not like this." Spring smiled ruefully. "Though God knows why I've chosen to fall in love—really in love, for the first time in my life—with Clay McEntire, of all people. I always thought I wanted a nice *normal* person. You know, one from the same planet?"

Summer chuckled, her blue eyes dancing with pleasure. "It has to be the way he dresses," she managed brokenly. "You just couldn't resist the pink suit."

That did it. Both of them fell back in their chairs and laughed hysterically at Clay's expense. And Spring felt much better when they'd finished. She found herself clinging to a foolish hope that she and Clay were going to be together long past the end of her vacation.

IT WASN'T going to work, Clay had decided by Monday morning. He shoved his fingers through his already disordered hair and stared glumly at the stacks of papers on his desk. His relationship with Spring wasn't going to work. He might as well acknowledge that now and start trying to accept it. Actually, he'd started accepting it yesterday, when he'd been away from her long enough to clear his love-clouded mind and take a long look at the situation. He was angry with himself because he hadn't even called her, as he'd promised. But he couldn't be objective when he was with her or even talking to her on the phone.

Spring loved her home state. She was happy there, happy with her career, her friends, having her parents within visiting distance. She'd made a success of her practice, and she'd worked hard to do it. She wouldn't be interested in giving it up and moving to San Francisco, where she'd have to start from scratch.

Besides, he asked himself honestly, leaning back in his comfortably worn desk chair and staring at the Mickey Mouse poster on his office wall, what did he have to offer her? He wasn't the most stable, settled person. He liked taking life one day at a time, living impulsively. He was unofficially on call at all hours for any troubled teenager who needed him; it wasn't unusual for him to receive calls in the middle of the night that had him jumping out of bed and running to help. His love and his energy were spent on his kids, and he wasn't sure how much was left over. Hadn't that been his reason for staying single all along? How did he know what kind of husband he'd make, assuming that he decided he wanted to marry Spring or she him?

He leaned his elbows on his desk and dropped his face into his hands. He loved her so much. He'd never imagined loving anyone this much. She was going to rip a part of him away when she left on Wednesday. But there was nothing he could do about it. He didn't feel right about asking her to stay, asking her to risk her future on him.

Another thought hit him, making him lift his head and rest his chin on his fists, frowning fiercely at old Mickey, as if the cartoon mouse had made the suggestion. Go with her? To Little Rock, Arkansas? He was California born and bred, quite comfortable with the fast lane. What was there for him in Little Rock? He wouldn't even be able to communicate with the kids there, much less help them. Would he? And what made him think she'd want him to go with her? She'd never said that she loved him, only that she was attracted to him. And that wasn't enough.

No. He slowly shook his head at Mickey, whom he fancied was beginning to wear a look of sympathy. Mick knew it wasn't going to work, too, he decided, trying to find his always present sense of humor. Even that didn't help. He didn't feel like laughing or even smiling. He felt like crying. Or going after Spring, kidnapping her to a desert island somewhere and making love to her thirty times a day until they both succumbed to exhaustion. Since he wasn't going to do either of those things, he decided to get back to work.

It was a long day. Students were in and out of his office in a steady stream. He'd heard from those who claimed their teachers picked on them, those whose parents didn't understand them, those madly in love and wanting advice or approval. Only now that school had been dismissed for the afternoon did he have some time alone to clear his desk. He pulled a file folder in front of him and began to go over the records of a recent transfer to the school, a boy who'd been in trouble at his former school in Oregon. And for the first time in years Clay found another person's problems having to compete with his own for his full attention.

8

SPRING HAD JUST PULLED the hem of her soft blue sweater over her slacks Monday night, in preparation for an evening at Connie's and Joel's, when her sister knocked, then peeked cautiously around the bedroom door. "Spring, Clay's here," Summer said almost hesitantly, knowing that Spring was upset because she hadn't heard from Clay since the wee hours of Sunday morning. "To be honest, he seems to be in a lousy mood."

He was in a bad mood? Spring was the one who was annoyed—with him, for the mixed signals that were so hard for her to understand, and with herself, for allowing things to become so awkward. Her heart curled up and whimpered, afraid it was about to be kicked. "Okay, I'm ready," she said impassively, hoping that her cool expression hid her anxiety.

Clay was waiting for her in the den. Summer and Derek had tactfully disappeared. Clay's smile was a bit strained when Spring entered the room. She clenched her hands in the pockets of her pleated slacks, hiding their trembling. "Hello, Clay."

"Hi, Spring." Even his voice sounded different somehow.

Only then did she notice what he was wearing, a bright turquoise leather bomber jacket over a baggy, multipocketed air-force-styled jumpsuit in neon yellow. Odd, she mused absently, how she noticed his clothing now only as an afterthought. She stood where she was, unsmiling, watching him. She had no intention of making things easier for him.

Clay made a sharp, impatient gesture, and then he was across the room and she was in his arms. "I'm sorry," he murmured into her hair, holding her so tightly that it hurt.

She didn't complain but burrowed into his shoulder, her hands clutching his back beneath the buttery-soft jacket. "Sorry about what?"

"For not calling you yesterday."

She shook her head against him. "You don't owe me explanations."

"I promised I'd call," he replied flatly. "At the very least, I owe you an apology."

She wanted so badly to ask why he hadn't called, but she couldn't, and he didn't volunteer the information. It wasn't as if he owed her anything or didn't deserve time away from her, she told herself. But he'd promised he'd call.

He kissed her rather roughly and set her a few inches away from him. "I thought you and I could follow Derek and Summer in my car to Connie's tonight, if that's okay with you," he said with obviously forced airiness.

Why are you acting so strangely? "Of course that's all right with me."

He nodded and turned to stare out the huge window of the den. He seemed distant, as if his thoughts were turned so deeply inward that he was having to make an effort to concentrate on anything going on around him. He'd been so open with her until now. It hurt to be shut out.

"Did you see Thelma today?" she asked him, struggling to make conversation.

He nodded. "Yes. They're moving her into a regular room tomorrow."

"That's good, isn't it? It means she's better." *Talk to me, Clay. Tell me what's bothering you.*

"Yes, she's much better. The doctors seem quite pleased with her progress."

"How is she emotionally?"

"She's okay. Her mother's no help, but her aunt Diane is here now, and she's very nice. I think she'll be able to help Thelma a great deal."

"I'm glad." And that was all she could think of to say. *If it's not Thelma, then what is it? Are you tired of me already? I'll only be here for two more days.* "I'll go see if Summer and Derek are ready."

Clay nodded, not even looking around at her as she left the room.

They were in the library-styled room that Derek used as an office at home, Summer leafing through a magazine as her husband glanced through some files at an enormous rolltop desk. She looked up curiously when Spring entered. "You and Clay ready to go? Tonight should be fun."

Spring nodded doubtfully. "I hope so."

"Uh-oh. He's still in a bad mood?"

"He's in an odd mood. A bit withdrawn."

Summer placed the magazine on a low table, looking thoughtful. "He gets that way sometimes. Usually when he's worried about something."

Spring thought wistfully of how little she actually knew about Clay. Summer knew him much better, even though Spring had made love with him. Why had she thought that the physical closeness they'd shared would bring them closer together emotionally, as well? Obviously she'd been wrong.

Clay paced the den, waiting for the others to join him. He knew that he'd confused Spring earlier, but he didn't know how else to act with her. He'd never been at such a loss. He loved her, he'd shared something with her that surpassed any experience he'd ever had with a woman, and yet there was still nothing more between them than . . . than a vacation affair, he thought sadly. She still planned to leave him in a couple of days, and he saw nothing for them beyond that time. *Dammit, how am I supposed to act?*

He looked up as Spring came back into the room and mentally flinched at the wary look on her pretty face. *Don't look at me like that, Spring. Don't you know I only want to hold you, love you? Can't you see that you're tearing me apart?*

He'd thought it would be easier in a larger group of people to ignore the panic that was steadily building within him and act naturally. Instead, being with Summer and Derek and Joel and Connie during the dinner that Connie and Joel had prepared for them was unexpectedly painful. The other couples were so happy, so comfortable in their relationships. Clay found himself noting each loving look and intimate touch that passed between them. He, on the other hand, was carefully avoiding meeting Spring's eyes or touching her more than necessary because he wasn't sure how well he could control his emotions. He supposed there was some ironic humor in the situation—a natural toucher such as himself envying others for being able to touch the ones they loved. Too bad he didn't feel like laughing. And why did he find himself getting so angry?

"So you'll be back in Little Rock by Wednesday evening," Joel was saying to Spring when Clay forced his attention to the conversation going on around him. "When do you go back to work?"

"Not until Monday," Spring answered. "I have some things I want to do around the house, so I took a full two weeks off—first time since I opened my practice almost two years ago."

"You're going to be busy when you get back," Summer commented. "I'll bet your patients will be lined up at the door Monday morning."

Spring smiled. "Well, actually, my appointment book is full for the next few weeks. But I'm not complaining about business being good."

"I thought we were going to watch a movie," Clay blurted out suddenly and not particularly graciously. He couldn't sit quietly and listen to them talk about Spring leaving. He winced at the wide-eyed looks of surprise turned his way and tried to make a joke. "I'm not allowed to stay up past ten on school nights."

"Sure, Clay. We really believe that," Connie retorted, but she stood and inserted the cassette into the VCR. With surreptitious glances at Clay that he didn't miss, the others settled back in their seats to watch the movie.

Spring's attention remained on Clay. He looked up to find her watching him with an expression that he couldn't read. Disgusted with himself for acting like a jerk, he reached out to take her hand, unable to resist raising it to his lips. Her skin was soft beneath his mouth, and he felt her pulse racing in her slender wrist at the caress. His own body responded. He wanted her. He remembered his earlier fantasy of picking her up, throwing her over his shoulder and carrying her off to an isolated spot. It still sounded good. And just as impossible.

He lowered their linked hands to his thigh and turned his gaze toward the big-screen television, trying to pay attention to the recently released comedy that he'd wanted to see at one time. Now he couldn't care less about the movie.

Anger. The doctor of psychology in him recognized the emotion as reaction to his upcoming loss, his dread of rejection. The neglected little boy still buried deep inside him was unable to rationalize the inappropriate emotion away. He was hurting, and it made him want to lash out at the cause of his pain—Spring.

What is wrong with him? Spring asked herself for the...well, she'd lost track of the number of times. *Why is he treating me this way? Almost like a stranger.*

She hadn't thought he'd be the type of man to lose interest once he'd made another conquest. Maybe she'd misjudged him.

He'd barely touched her this evening. After all the touching he'd done from the moment they'd met, now he seemed to have no problem at all keeping his hands to himself. He was holding her hand now, but it seemed almost an afterthought to him, almost as if he were doing her a favor, she thought resentfully.

Was Saturday night your idea of a favor, Clay? Were you just going along with Summer's brilliant idea of providing some excitement for her bored older sister? She uncurled her fingers from his and clenched her hands in her lap. *Don't do me any more favors, Clay.*

The catalyst for seething emotion came after the movie, when the three couples were talking over nightcaps before breaking up for the evening. The talk had turned, as it so often did, to Halloran House and its residents. Summer had spent part of the afternoon there and was telling the others about something that had happened to upset some of the young people. It seemed that a fourteen-year-old friend of theirs had run away from home after a quarrel with his parents. The parents had sent the police after him. They'd found him in a bus station, preparing to leave town.

"The kids were really upset because the police made a very public thing out of dragging Tony out of the bus station. It was all terribly humiliating for him," Summer added.

Clay scowled. "I hadn't heard about that." Great. He'd been so wrapped up in Spring that he hadn't even known that one of his kids had been in trouble. *Thanks a lot, Spring.*

"The kids are all furious with Tony's parents," Summer told him, fluffing her long bangs, a habitual gesture.

Spring shifted in her seat. "What else could the parents have done? It wasn't their fault that the police were overly enthusiastic in carrying out their jobs."

"They could have gone after their son themselves, rather than sending the cops," Clay answered, standing and looking down at her as if she weren't very bright, she thought resentfully. "Or they could have called Frank or me. We could have found him."

"I only know that if my son had run away, I'd do exactly what Tony's parents did. After all, if the police had been able to find Thelma earlier, she wouldn't have been so close to death by the time you got to her."

"And if her mother had called me sooner, I'd have found her earlier," Clay argued. "The cops never would have found her at all, the way they were going. It was probably just an accident that they found Tony."

"You mean everyone in San Francisco should call you when their kids run away?" Was he really so arrogant?

He flushed at the derision in her tone, shoving his hands in his pockets. "Not everyone, of course. But if I happen to know the kids and work with them, as I have with Thelma and Tony, it would seem only logical to give me a chance to help. Hell, I didn't even know Tony had run away until just now." His tone clearly implied that it was Spring's fault that he hadn't known—quite unfairly, she thought, piqued.

"Maybe they decided to try something new, if you've been working with him and he still ran away." *Oops, wrong choice of words. I might as well have come right out and accused Clay of failing with Tony,* she realized when his face hardened. She opened her mouth to clarify the statement, but Summer jumped in hastily to change the subject, obviously hoping to avoid the confrontation that was building between Spring and Clay.

"It's getting late," Clay said abruptly, still glaring at Spring. "Are you ready to go?"

She nodded. "Yes. I'm ready."

Spring was rather surprised when Clay told Derek and Summer that he'd take her home later. After their near quarrel she expected him to take her straight back to Sausalito. Instead, she found herself walking on a beach with him about half an hour after leaving the others, huddling into the windbreaker she'd worn with her slacks and sweater as the damp, cool, salted breeze tossed her hair and reddened her cheeks.

Clay kicked at a broken shell, then bent to pick it up and toss it into the waves breaking nearby. "Tonight wasn't much fun for you, was it?"

She took a deep breath and stopped walking, turning to face him squarely. "You didn't seem to be enjoying yourself, either."

"No, I guess I wasn't." His face was deeply shadowed in the fog-diffused moonlight. "I'm sorry."

Her chest hurt. She thought it might be because her heart was being thoroughly pummeled. "What's wrong, Clay?" she finally found the courage to ask. *Please talk to me.*

"What's wrong?" He shoved his fingers through his windblown hair, staring impassively at her as he appeared to debate his reply. When he finally spoke, his voice was raw. "I'm going to miss you, Spring. I'll miss you very much."

She let her head drop forward. "I'll miss you, too, Clay," she whispered. But he hadn't asked her to stay, nor would she be the one to suggest it. How could she, when she wasn't at all sure that she wanted to stay in San Francisco? As much as she'd enjoyed her visit, she was already homesick. As much as she dreaded leaving Clay, she still rather looked forward to getting back to work on Monday. God, what a mess she'd made of everything! "Oh, Clay."

He caught her in his arms and held her tightly. "Dammit, Spring. Don't you know that you've disrupted my entire life? I haven't been able to think about anything but you since you arrived. My kids, my job, my friends—I forget them all when you're around. That's never happened to me before."

"I haven't tried to come between you and your work," she murmured, clinging tightly to him.

"I know that. I haven't forgotten that I practically had to kidnap you to go out with me." Even that was said with resentment. Spring blinked back tears.

"Clay, what do you want from me?" she asked at last, tilting her head back to look up at him. "I don't know what you want me to do or say."

"No." And this time his voice was sad. "You don't know me, do you? You don't even know how much I—" he stopped, swallowed, then went on a little too smoothly "—how much I care for you."

She didn't know what to say, so she remained quiet, clinging to him. His turquoise leather jacket was damp and smooth beneath her cheek, his arms hard and strong around her. And despite his current moodiness making him almost a stranger to her, she loved him.

Clay pressed his mouth to her temple. "Kiss me, Spring."

She lifted her head, her hands going up to pull his mouth down to hers. It seemed like so long since he'd kissed her. He brushed his lips lingeringly across hers, then deepened the kiss. He groaned thickly when her lips parted to invite him inside, his hands tightening to lift her against him. "Spring," he muttered into the depths of her mouth. "Oh, God, Spring, I...I want you so much."

"Then what are we doing on this beach?" she asked huskily, straining to press closer—a physical impossibility with the barrier of clothing between them.

He shuddered when she arched her lower body suggestively into his, then set her firmly away from him. "It's late," he said, his voice hoarse. "I'd better take you home."

She blinked in dismay at the abrupt end of the caress. She'd thought the kiss was leading to something further, that he'd take her back to his house and make love to her again. Why wasn't he? Not because he didn't want her—they'd been in much too close proximity for him to hide his desire for her. She'd never been the instigator of lovemaking, but she wanted Clay so much. She had so little time left with him. "I hope you mean your home," she blurted out bravely.

"No. I mean your sister's home." He half turned away from her, his hands going into the pockets of his neon-yellow jumpsuit. "It *is* getting late, and I have to work tomorrow."

He might as well have slapped her. Spring lowered her head so that her hair fell forward to hide her face and walked slowly beside him, back to his car. Her eyes smarted with tears, but she refused to shed them. They'd parted so sweetly during the wee hours of Sunday morning. She hadn't expected such awkwardness and confusion their next time together. *Damn you, Clay, why are you punishing me? What have I done, other than fall in love with you?*

Neither of them made even a pretense of talking on the drive back to Summer's house. Clay probably would have just walked her to the door and driven away had not Summer and Derek driven up at almost the same time. "We stopped for cherry cheesecake and coffee," Summer explained as the four of them walked toward the front door together. "I didn't think you'd be home until much later," she added to Spring, her eyebrow arching questioningly at their strained expressions.

"Clay has to work tomorrow," Spring replied, using Clay's own excuse. It sounded just as hollow coming from her, she decided wearily.

"Clay, I forgot to give you the proposal you asked for on doing a theatrical production with the Halloran House kids. I have it ready," Summer told him. "Want to come in and let me get it?"

Though he looked anxious to leave, Clay agreed to
come in only long enough for Summer to retrieve the
papers. The telephone was ringing when they entered;
the call was for Derek, a late business call that he decided to take in his study.

"I was hoping that Tony would take a part in the
play," Summer said before going off to look for the
proposal for Clay. "He's been so interested in the drama
classes we've done at Halloran House. Now I don't
know if he'll be able to stay with us."

"Thanks to his parents calling in the cops," Clay
muttered, darting an eloquent look at Spring as Summer left the room with a promise to hurry back.

Spring lifted her chin defiantly, still seething at his
rejection on the beach and annoyed with his persis-
tence in arguing with her viewpoint about this boy she'd
never even met. *What does this have to do with us,
anyway?* she asked herself, even as she felt compelled
to respond to his challenge. "If they hadn't called the
police, he still wouldn't be in your play," she pointed out
coolly. "Who knows where he would be by now?"

"You still think they did the right thing, don't you?
Even after I explained my viewpoint."

"Yes, I do," she insisted. "I realize that you are an expert in this field, *Dr.* McEntire, but even you are not
infallible."

Clay stiffened, his eyes kindling with the smoldering
anger that had seemed just below the surface all evening. "I never said I was infallible."

"No, just that you're always right, is that it?" Spring
snapped. She glared fiercely at the man who'd turned
her inside out over the past few days. "It's easy for you
to say what parents should do or how they should raise

their children. It's always easy for people who don't have children to tell others how to raise them."

"I suppose you know better?" he demanded, almost in a yell. "Hell, you've never even *been* a child! You were born being the responsible older sister, weren't you, *Dr.* Reed?"

Spring went cold with fury. How *dare* this . . . this perpetual adolescent criticize her? *She* certainly wasn't the one acting like an unreasonable stranger! "I like to think that I'm a responsible person. When I make promises, I try to keep them. I know, for example, that if I promised to call someone, I would certainly do so." *Now talk to me, Clay. Tell me why you didn't call. Why you're angry tonight. Ask me to stay in San Francisco.*

"My not calling you has absolutely nothing to do with this!" Clay protested heatedly, though he'd flushed at her pointed accusation. "We're talking about a young man's dignity here."

"And of course you're the expert on dignity." Spring eyed his fluorescent clothing as she voiced the disdainful comment, lashing out at him from the depths of hurt and confusion and heartsick love. She was sorry almost immediately, but something kept her apology inside her. She only stared at him, knowing that she had just destroyed anything that might have remained between them.

Clay's face went white. "Maybe you're right," he replied rather hoarsely. "I'm not the one who tries to live according to everyone else's rules of duty and responsibility and propriety. You've believed from the beginning that I was too much of a nonconformist for you, haven't you? An irresponsible, immature playboy who dresses funny—does that sum up your opinion of me, *Dr.* Reed? Fine. If that's what you want to believe, go ahead. I'm quite content with my life and the accomplishments I've made and will make in the future. You can go back to your Rogers in their plain ties and suits and socks and see if they can make you happy. Personally, I don't think you will be because you'll never find a man who quite measures up to your idea of mature, responsible perfection!"

And with that final, softly spoken, heart-slashing pronouncement he turned and walked with undeniable dignity out of the room. Even from the den Spring heard the front door slam behind him.

"Spring, what in the world happened? I've never seen Clay look so furious!" With Derek following just behind her, Summer entered the room and rushed to her sister's side, her lovely, expressive face creased with concern.

"I don't want to talk about it, Summer."

"But—"

Spring whirled on her younger sister with barely suppressed violence. "I said I *don't* want to talk about it!"

Derek stepped in quickly to prevent the sibling confrontation that threatened. "I think it would be best if you let it drop, Summer," he said gently. "Spring can tell you about it when she calms down, if she wants to then."

Feeling numb and clinging desperately to that blessed numbness, Spring forced a smile. "Thank you, Derek. Now if you'll excuse me, I think I'll turn in."

She felt the anxious eyes of her sister and brother-in-law on her as she left the room, but she kept her shoulders straight, her pace unhurried. And her mind blank.

CLAY STORMED into his house, walked to his bar for the second time in two days and, for the first time since he'd been in college, deliberately set out to get drunk. Unfortunately, it didn't work. He kept replaying his fight with Spring and forgetting his drink until finally he set the barely touched tumbler on the bar and began to restlessly pace the room.

He might as well admit that he'd been spoiling for a fight tonight. He just hadn't known it at the time. And, from all appearances, Spring had been just as eager to lash out at him.

Of course, all she'd said was that she would have called the police if it had been her son who'd run away. She couldn't know how Tony must have felt, couldn't understand the kinds of pressures and torments that would make a young man feel compelled to leave the safety of his home and face the streets alone. It was a degrading, humiliating experience being treated like a mindless child, forced to face the problems he'd run away from whether he was ready to do so or not.

But, dammit, how dare she argue with him about one of his kids? Couldn't she at least have given him credit to know his own field? He had a goddamned doctorate in adolescent psychology, he thought bleakly, and she had accused him of knowing nothing about kids simply because he hadn't fathered any!

Maybe it was best just to let it end this way. He hoped that his friendship with Summer wouldn't be affected after Spring left. He was going to need that friendship now more than he ever had before.

Yes, best to let it end. Before they hurt each other even more than they already had.

He dropped his chin to his chest. *Oh, God, Spring. Don't leave me.*

SPRING FOLDED the last item of clothing and placed it neatly in her suitcase, then closed the lid and firmly snapped the locks. Another suitcase sat at her feet and beside it a third, borrowed from Summer. She was taking home quite a bit more than she'd arrived with, thanks to those pleasant shopping trips she and her sister had made during her visit. She only wished she'd spent more time with her sister and less time with the man who'd managed to break her heart, she thought sorrowfully, then immediately called herself a liar. No matter how deep the pain of her loss, and it was agonizingly deep, she couldn't bring herself to regret one moment of the time she'd spent with Clay.

"I have one more thing for you to take home with you," Summer announced from the doorway, entering the room with her oddly graceful limp. In her arms she bore a large, battered Winnie the Pooh.

Spring smiled in surprise. "Pooh Bear! Gosh, I haven't seen him in years."

"Still looks great, doesn't he?" Summer asked, fondly eyeing the badly bedraggled stuffed toy. "Considering that he was yours, then mine, then Autumn's, it's a miracle that he's still in one piece. Well, mostly in one piece."

"Yes, he's still missing an ear, thanks to our fiery-tempered baby sister. How did he end up in California?"

"Autumn gave him back to me when I left Arkansas. She didn't want me to be lonely. Now I want you to take him back to Arkansas for the same reason. He's a great friend."

Spring had determined right after her quarrel with Clay that she wouldn't cry in front of her sister, but she found herself forcing back tears at Summer's gesture. "All right, I'll take him," she said softly. "Thanks."

Summer nodded. "Derek's ready to leave for the airport anytime you are. Sure you don't want me to go along?"

"No, you have your class late this afternoon, and there's no need for you to miss it. You've skipped enough classes while I've been here."

"None that really mattered."

"Still, it's better this way. I hate airport goodbyes."

"Me, too," Summer confessed. "You'll call?"

"I'll call. And write."

"You'd better." Summer reached out and hugged her sister fiercely. "I love you, Sis. I'm so glad you came."

"Me, too." Spring returned the hug with equal vehemence. "Your husband is a terrific guy, Summer Anderson. I'm very happy for you both."

"Spring..." Summer hesitated, then spoke bravely. "Why don't you call him?"

Spring immediately shook her head. "No."

"Are you still that angry with him?"

"No." It was true; she wasn't. She knew how deeply he cared about his kids. She still thought she'd been entitled to her own opinion, but she saw Clay's point, too. And, she added sadly, if he'd wanted to talk to her, he would have called. "No, I'm not angry. But it's better this way."

And it was, she tried to convince herself on the way to the airport. The relationship between her and Clay had been ill-fated from the beginning. She'd known from her first glance at him that, though he was attractive and fascinating, he wasn't for her. But, God, it hurt.

"You're really going to hold that bear all the way to Little Rock?" Derek asked doubtfully as Spring prepared to board her plane. She'd checked her other luggage, but she clung to Pooh with gentle determination.

"Yes. We'll be fine, Derek."

"Sure?" His raw, deep voice was gentle, as were his searching pewter-gray eyes.

"Yes, I'm sure."

"Spring." He took her forearms in his large hands and looked down at her. "I just want you to know that I think you and Clay are being a couple of first-class idiots. I know when two people are in love, and you and Clay are. Don't let pride stand between you."

She winced. "Derek, I know you're only trying to help, but you're wrong. Clay and I just don't work together. We're not right for each other. I'm not what he needs, and he's not— He's . . ." But that was one lie she couldn't voice. "Please, Derek," she said finally on a sigh.

"All right." He kissed her fondly on the cheek. "You keep in touch."

"I will. And I'll see you when you bring Summer home for Christmas. Remember, you promised."

"Right. See you then. If not before," he added somewhat mysteriously.

Spring turned for one last, lingering look around the crowded terminal before boarding her plane, ostensibly as a last glance at San Francisco. If she'd secretly hoped to spot a shaggy blond head or a man dressed in outrageous style, she tried not to acknowledge it, even to herself.

9

"DON'T DROP THE PIZZA!" Kelsey Rayford, Spring's office manager and best friend, cried out in teasing warning as Spring balanced the enormous white box while unlocking the door to her apartment.

"I've got the pizza, you hang on to the wine," Spring returned with a grin, triumphantly swinging open the door to her roomy west Little Rock town-house apartment. Offering a cheerful greeting to the small yellow-and-white cat that had dashed to greet her, she crossed immediately to a round oak table and deposited the fragrant, still warm box on it, then dropped her purse on a chair and turned to her friend.

Tiny, black-haired, brown-eyed Kelsey laughed as she juggled a large bottle of wine, an enormous handbag and a sizable, gaily wrapped package. "I'm losing the wine. Grab it!"

Spring grabbed, catching the bottle just as it would have plunged to the floor. "If you wouldn't insist on carrying a purse that would hold half the contents of our office filing cabinets, you wouldn't have this problem," she lectured primly.

"Oh, stuff it," her friend replied inelegantly, dropping the maligned purse to the floor. "Just because you're older than me doesn't mean you can start giving lectures."

"Hey, I'm not that much older! Three days doesn't count."

Grinning at Spring's protest, Kelsey shook her head. "Sorry. For the next three days you're twenty-seven and I'm a mere twenty-six. I intend to point that out at every opportunity."

"Somehow I knew you would," Spring retorted, rummaging in her cabinets for plates and wineglasses.

The doorbell chimed and Spring turned over the duty of setting the table to Kelsey. Her neighbor, Mrs. English, stood on the doorstep, arms loaded with packages. "You had a few deliveries today, Spring."

"I can see that." Spring smiled and took the load. "Would you like to come in for a while, Mrs. English?"

"No, thanks, hon. Tom will be home for his dinner shortly. Hope you have a happy birthday."

"Thank you."

"Oh, goody, presents," Kelsey crooned when Mrs. English had gone. "And such nice big ones."

"I can't believe they all arrived on my birthday." Spring eyed the three brown-paper-wrapped parcels with interest. Trust her family to make sure she had birthday presents, she thought fondly.

"Well, are you going to open them?" Kelsey demanded impatiently. Kelsey was always impatient.

Spring shook her head. "After dinner. Our pizza will get cold if we don't eat it now."

Sighing, Kelsey reached for a plate. "I don't know how you can stand it. I'd have ripped into them the minute I got them."

"Yes, but you've never understood the pleasure to be found in deferred gratification," Spring pointed out indulgently, seating herself across the table from her friend.

"Oh, God, now you're talking like my shrink." The animated brunette stared soulfully over a half-eaten triangle of pizza. "You'd think you were a psychologist rather than an optometrist."

Psychologist. Even the word made Spring wince. "Eat your pizza, Kelsey."

Spring chatted gaily during the casual dinner—but then, she'd become an expert on hiding her feelings behind airy chatter during the past two months. She and Kelsey talked about the office, about the volunteer work that Spring had recently taken on at a local resident treatment home for troubled young people, about the gorgeous-but-just-not-real-bright man that Kelsey had dated a couple of times recently. And though Spring mentioned her sisters frequently and occasionally referred to her trip to California, she never once spoke of a tall, golden-haired man with blue-green eyes and a brilliant white smile. She had not spoken Clay's name since she'd returned to Little Rock.

"I don't know how you do it," Kelsey murmured as they finished the pizza and lingered over a last glass of wine.

"Do what?" Spring asked lazily, feeding a tiny bite of pizza crust to Missy, her cat.

"Stay so busy all the time. You were a workaholic before your vacation, but since you've been back, you're going all the time. To be honest, I'm starting to worry about you."

Few people would have been able to tell that Spring's smile was forced. She devoutly hoped that Kelsey wasn't one of those people. "Why in the world would you worry about me? I'm doing fine."

Rich brown eyes studied her face with an intensity that almost made Spring squirm. "I don't know what it is," Kelsey said finally, "but something's been different about you ever since you got back from visiting your sister. I've asked you repeatedly if anything happened while you were away, but you always shrug off my questions. Are you sure you don't want to talk to me about anything?"

"Kelsey, when did you become such a worrier? Haven't I always been able to take care of myself?"

"You're not going to talk about it, are you?"

Deliberately avoiding those searching eyes, Spring shrugged. "I don't know about you, but I'm ready to see what's in those packages. Deferred gratification is all very well, but it's time for birthday presents."

"You can be a real pain sometimes, Spring Reed," Kelsey muttered, but her attention had already strayed to the tantalizing birthday presents. She might be close to twenty-seven, but Kelsey Rayford did love presents—even if they were someone else's, as Spring knew very well.

"I'll open yours first." Spring reached for the colorful package that Kelsey had brought in earlier and tugged at the ribbon. The box opened to reveal a sheer, lace-trimmed nightgown in swirls of pastels. "Kelsey, thank you. It's lovely."

"It'll look great on you. I'm hoping it'll give you the incentive to find someone special to wear it for."

Avoiding her friend's mischievous grin, Spring began to open the box from Florida. She reflected somberly that it was a good thing she enjoyed wearing pretty nightgowns just for herself; she had no plans to wear the garment for anyone else. She couldn't imagine being that close again to any man but—

No. She wouldn't even think about him. She ripped the paper from Autumn's gift with unnecessary force, then laughed when she opened it and saw a heavy-duty lavender plastic case fitted with a set of tools—hammer, screwdrivers, pliers, wrenches, tape measure. A woman's tool kit. How typically Autumn. Defiantly functional, yet somehow feminine. "Now this will come in handy."

"You must have told Autumn that you're thinking of buying a house. You won't have a manager then to take care of repairs for you."

"I've discussed it with her. She agreed that it would be a good investment."

Kelsey looked around Spring's rose-and-cream apartment, carefully decorated with Victorian antiques and reproductions, and sighed. "I don't know how you could even think of giving up this place. It's so beautiful and you don't have to worry about lawns and plumbing and peeling paint."

Spring shrugged. "I like it here, but I've always wanted to own my own house. Don't ask why; it's just a personal whim. Besides, these furnishings are mine. My house would look a lot like this."

"True. Open the others."

Amused at Kelsey's childlike excitement, Spring obliged, tearing the paper off a package from the West Coast to reveal a large, flat box. Her breath caught in her throat when she lifted layers of tissue paper to reveal a painting. *The* painting. The one she'd seen in the boutique in Sausalito of the intricately depicted Victorian house surrounded by flowers, with just a suggestion of San Francisco Bay in the background.

Oh, Summer, why?

"Spring, it's beautiful! It goes perfectly with all your things. Gosh, look at the detail of that house. It's— Spring, what's the matter? Don't you like it?"

Spring cleared her throat and blinked, pushing her glasses up onto the bridge of her nose as she pasted on a smile and looked at Kelsey. "Of course I like it. I saw it in an art gallery in Sausalito and fell in love with it then. I was just . . . touched that Summer and Derek bought it for me."

"Oh." Kelsey frowned, still watching Spring closely, obviously suspecting that she hadn't been told the entire story.

Spring hadn't cried since she'd returned from California. Not that she hadn't wanted to, but she couldn't. The pain was too deep for tears. She refused to cry now. Tossing her head, she lifted the smaller package, barely looking at it as she fought to hold on to her enthusiasm for her birthday presents. She pushed at her glasses again and smoothed back a curl that had escaped from her prim roll of hair. She'd worn her hair up every day for the past two months.

"Oh!" The delicate gold bracelet was exquisite, engraved with an old-fashioned pattern of birds and flowers. It could have come straight from the early 1800s. It suited her perfectly. From her parents? Spring lifted the small white card enclosed in the box, read the four words written on it and dropped it with a strangled cry.

Happy birthday, sweet Spring.

"Oh, no," she whispered, her body curling inward and her eyes closing with the pain. "Oh, Clay, why?"

She'd tried so hard not to think of him. She'd stayed busy, kept her mind occupied. And it had worked—during the days, at least. Only during the nights had he haunted her. Endless, empty nights filled with laughing eyes, lazy, bright smiles, thick golden hair. A deep breath, and she could imagine herself in his arms, held close to his pounding heart as he loved her with a hungry tenderness that had surpassed any fantasy she'd ever had. And then she'd open her eyes and she'd be alone. But she hadn't cried.

She still regretted their quarrel. Though she could understand now that the argument had been the result of their precarious emotions regarding their impending separation, she wished they could have parted on better terms. They'd said some terrible, hurtful things to each other. She hoped that someday he could forgive her, as she had already forgiven him. And it seemed that he had. But it still hurt.

If only she knew how to get over him. Would there ever come a time when she could think about him without this horrible pain? When spotting a tall blond male in a crowd would not cause her heart to stop? When she'd stop thinking of amusing incidents she'd like to share with him? She had tried; God, she had tried. And she still loved him. Just as she always would.

"Spring? Spring, are you all right?" Kelsey's voice came from unexpected proximity.

Spring opened her eyes to find her friend kneeling in front of her, brown eyes huge with concern. "Spring, what's wrong?" Kelsey asked again.

Spring wet her lips, took a deep breath and sat up straight. "It's...nothing, Kelsey. I..." She stopped and buried her face in her hands, unable to lie. "Everything's wrong," she wailed, the tears finally beginning to flow.

"Only a man could cause this kind of heartache," Kelsey pronounced confidently, her hand on her friend's shoulder. "I'm speaking from experience. Who is he, Spring? Not Roger. You never looked like this over him."

Shaking her head, Spring dropped her hands. "No, not Roger."

"Ready to talk about it?"

"His name is Clay McEntire. He's . . ." How did one describe Clay? "He's tall and blond and has blue-green eyes and a beautiful smile. He's a junior-high-school counselor who loves kids and tears himself up over their problems. He wears funny clothes and likes to tease and shows his affection for his friends through hugs and touches. He had a lot of problems when he was young, but he overcame them. He's sometimes moody and...and he needs reading glasses, but I don't think he knows it," she finished with a sob.

Kelsey was staring at her in unmistakable astonishment. "He, um, he sounds fascinating. Not your usual type, though."

Spring choked on a humorless laugh. "No. Not my usual type."

"But you're in love with him."

"Completely. Forever."

"And?"

"And nothing. He's in San Francisco and I'm in Little Rock."

"Is he in love with you?"

"I don't know," Spring answered slowly, twisting the lovely gold bracelet between shaking hands. "I just don't know. There were times when I thought he might be. When he— When we— Well, he made me feel very special. But, for all I know, that may be the way he treats every woman in his life."

"So this is why you've been driving yourself like a madwoman ever since you got back." Kelsey shook her head in reproval. "I can't believe you've been carrying this around inside you without even telling me about it."

"I just couldn't talk about it. It still hurts too much."

"What do you think the bracelet means?"

"I don't know. Maybe it's just his way of apologizing for the quarrel we had before I left."

"Are you going to keep it?"

She hadn't thought that far ahead. Of course the logical thing to do would be to return it. It was, after all, much too expensive a gift and would only serve as a painful reminder of an incident best forgotten, she told herself. Her fingers tightened around the bangle almost in protest at the thought of sending it back. Clay had chosen this gift for her. Sending it back would almost be like saying goodbye again. "I don't know."

"When it comes to this guy, you don't know much, do you, Spring?" Kelsey asked with sympathetic amusement. "I think you should keep it."

"You do? Why?"

"Because he obviously wanted you to have it. And because he sounds like a great guy."

"He is." Spring brushed another wave of tears off her cheeks. "Oh, Kelsey, he is."

"Tell you what we're going to do." Kelsey pushed herself to her feet, rising to her entire four feet eleven inches. "We're going to drag out everything fattening in your kitchen, cover it all with whipped cream and pig out while you tell me every detail of your vacation in California—and this time you're not leaving out a guy named Clay McEntire, you hear?"

"Oh, Kelsey, I don't think—"

"Spring, trust me. Talking about it will help. Keeping it all in will only rot your insides."

Spring gave an unwilling smile, already feeling a little better. Kelsey had always had this effect on her, ever since the two had attended the same church as kids. Kelsey had grown up in Romance, Arkansas, just down the road from Spring's hometown of Rose Bud. They'd considered themselves quite cosmopolitan when they'd moved fifty-five miles south to the big city of Little Rock—population 194,000 at last count—Spring, after her graduation from optometry college almost two years earlier, and Kelsey, after her divorce a year before that. Kelsey had quit a good job to work for Spring, and the relationship had proven quite satisfying, both personally and professionally.

Spring left out no detail of the brief affair with Clay. From that first kiss in the hallway on the night they'd met to the scathing quarrel in Summer's den on that last Monday night, Spring poured out the entire story to her warmly sympathetic, if rather startled, friend. Kelsey had been right. It *did* feel good to talk about it.

"And that's the end of the story," she concluded, toying with a last bite of a sinfully gooey chocolate-fudge brownie sans whipped cream.

Kelsey looked thoughtful as she licked a bit of chocolate from her scarlet-tipped finger. "Somehow I don't think it is."

"What do you mean?"

"I don't happen to think the story's over. From what you've told me, Clay is as deeply involved in this relationship as you are. And he sent you that bracelet. I don't think he's going to let you go that easily."

"Let me go? Kelsey, he did everything but drive me to the airport and throw me on the plane."

"Mmm. We'll see."

"It's over, Kel."

Kelsey only shook her dark head. "Want to bet?"

"The last time I made a bet with you, you took my grandmother's earrings from me."

"I warned you not to bet them, didn't I? But you just wouldn't believe that you and Roger would break up in less than six months."

"Okay, so you were right about Roger."

"I'm right about this, too. I think I'll give you your grandmother's earrings as a wedding present."

Spring flinched. "Kelsey, don't, please. It did help to talk to you, but I can't joke about that."

Kelsey smiled sweetly. "I wasn't joking, Spring."

She left soon afterward since both of them had to work the next day. When she was alone, Spring hung the painting from Summer and Derek in a place of honor in her living room, telling herself that someday she'd be able to look at it without fighting tears. Then she folded the nightgown from Kelsey into a dresser drawer and stored the tool kit from Autumn in the kitchen pantry. Only then did she allow herself to pick up the bracelet again. Very slowly she clasped it around her wrist. It fit as if it had been made for her.

Holding her wrist to her cheek, she closed tear-flooded eyes and admitted to herself that she would not return the gift to its sender. She supposed she'd known that all along. She would wear the bracelet always, and every time she looked at it she would remember a very special man in California. The man who'd taught her how to love.

The telephone rang just as she was about to go to bed, hoping that she would be able to sleep. It was Summer, calling to wish her happy birthday, the last of her family to call that day.

"The painting is beautiful," Spring told her honestly. "I love it. Thank you."

"You're welcome. I could tell you really liked it when you saw it. I wanted you to have it. It's perfect for you."

Yes, it was perfect for her. Even though it made her cry. "How are you, Summer? And Derek?"

"We're fine. Connie and Joel were married last weekend, you know. It was a small ceremony, very sweet. Connie and I cried all the way through it. Derek acted like we were being very silly, but I saw him wipe his eyes once. He's denied it ever since, but I know what I saw."

"I'm very... happy for them," Spring managed, though there was a break in her voice.

"Clay was there, too."

"Oh." *Don't, Summer. Please.*

"I don't see him as much now as I did before. He's staying very busy these days."

"Is he?"

"Oh, Spring, you're miserable, aren't you? And I know he is, too. If only you'd seen his face during that wedding. He looked so unhappy."

"Summer, he knows where I am, how to get in touch with me. If . . . if he wanted a relationship with me, he would call." Instead, he'd sent her a bracelet and a card that only wished her a happy birthday. Nothing more.

"I think he's scared of the way you made him feel."

"Maybe he was. But whatever the reason, he's the one who ended it. I'm not going to chase after him, Summer. I can't. And, please, don't say anything to him. Please."

"I won't. He wouldn't let me, anyway. Like you, he refuses to talk about it. I'm so sorry, Spring."

"So am I. But I'll get over it." Maybe. Like when she was too old to remember.

"Happy birthday, Sis."

"Thanks for calling, Summer."

She hung up the phone and buried her face in her hands, her shoulders shaking with the force of her sobs.

Happy birthday, sweet Spring.

IT HADN'T BEEN ONE of her better days. It was ninety-seven degrees on this second Monday in July, the humidity was hovering at eighty-three percent and the air conditioner in Spring's offices had gone out. A frantic call had been put in to the repairman, but he hadn't shown up yet. Thanks to one woman who'd insisted on telling Spring her entire history of eye problems, covering some sixty-five years, Spring was running a bit late with her appointments. There were people sweltering in the waiting room, a small child was crying lustily as he waited for his brother to be fitted for glasses and the telephone hadn't stopped ringing all day.

Kelsey's dark hair was damp around her flushed face as she scrambled to keep up with calls and appointments. Spring's assistant, Andi, was dashing from one examining room to the other and Spring was trying to convince a very vain young woman that her particular vision problem did not lend itself to contact lenses. The woman left in a huff, informing Spring that she would get a second opinion.

"She'll find someone who'll fit her for contacts, you know," Andi predicted glumly.

"Yes, I know. And she'll be sorry later." Spring sighed as she swept a damp tendril of limp silvery hair back from her own glasses, which were causing her face to sweat. At times like this she considered getting contact lenses herself. The main reason she hadn't was because she thought they were just too much trouble. "Is the repairman here yet?"

"Yes, he just walked in. Kelsey took him straight to the compressor and told him she'd chain him to it if he didn't have it working in half an hour or less."

Spring laughed tiredly. "Sounds like Kelsey. How many more do we have?"

Andi checked the clipboard she held. "Mrs. Gray is in Room One. Needs a new prescription for her reading glasses. I just took Danny Gipson into Two. His glasses are in; you just need to fit them. We've got one more waiting in the lobby—a woman in her twenties who's been having headaches. Oh, and there's one last appointment due later, but he's not here yet."

"Maybe he'll be running late, too, and he won't have to wait in this heat. Do you have Mrs. Gray's file with you?"

Twenty minutes later Spring sat back on her stool, smiling with satisfaction at the seven-year-old boy grinning back at her, two of his front teeth notably absent. His freckled face was now enhanced by a stylish pair of glasses, through which his green eyes sparkled. "I see good through these, Dr. Reed," he informed her.

"That's great, Danny. Now you'll start making home runs every time you're up to bat, I'll bet."

He chuckled in pleasure. "Well, sometimes, maybe. I sure was glad to find out I'm not a klutz. Just blind."

Spring wrinkled her nose at him and affectionately ruffled his sandy hair, causing the gold bracelet on her wrist to sparkle in the bright office lighting. "You're not blind, Danny. You're just a little nearsighted. It happens to the best of us." She tapped her own plastic frames.

"Am I done now, Dr. Reed?"

"Yes, you are. What's your hurry?"

"I gotta go beat up Bobby Clary."

Spring's eyes widened in surprise. "Why would you want to beat up Bobby Clary?" she demanded.

"'Cause he's gonna call me 'Four Eyes,'" Danny replied happily. "See ya, Dr. Reed," he added, scrambling out of the examining chair.

"Don't break those glasses, Danny!" she called after him. Something told her she'd be seeing quite a bit of Danny.

The repairman had worked some kind of magic with the air conditioner, and already the offices were feeling cooler. Spring sighed in relief as she stepped into her office half an hour later after seeing her next-to-last patient. "Did our final appointment ever arrive?" she asked Andi.

"He's in Room Two." Andi rolled her expressive blue eyes. "And is he something! Kelsey's already given him her phone number."

Spring groaned dramatically and straightened her glasses. "What am I going to have to do to keep her from chasing after my patients?" she asked teasingly, glad to know that Kelsey's flirtatiousness remained within the bounds of good taste—while in the office, anyway. "What's this guy's name?"

Andi checked her clipboard. "Mr. Crowe. He's dressed kind of loud, but he's totally hot. Wait until you see him. Need any help?"

"I think I can manage, thank you." Spring's smile had faded a bit at the description of the man's clothing. Tiny reminders like that hurt, even after four months. Clay was still as firmly entrenched in her mind and heart as he'd been the night they'd made love, even though she hadn't heard another thing from him since the arrival of the bracelet she'd worn every day since her birthday.

Spring checked her appearance in a wall mirror before going in for her final appointment of the trying day. Her hair was still pinned up, though the tendrils that had escaped had frizzed a bit from the humid heat. Her makeup had long since faded from perspiration. The white lab coat she wore as a uniform over her plum cotton shirtdress was badly wrinkled. She looked as if she'd just put in a long, hard day. Oh, well, she thought in rueful resignation, it was just as well that she wasn't interested in the "hot" man waiting in Room Two. Kelsey could have him.

Donning her most professional smile, Spring strode briskly into Room Two, then stopped short, staring at the man in the examining chair. "Oh, my God."

"Awed reverence isn't necessary," her patient responded gravely, watching her with warm blue-green eyes. "You can just call me Clay."

Over a bright blue T-shirt he was wearing the wildest tropical print shirt she'd ever seen—huge parrots and oleanders in red, yellow, blue, hot pink and white—with red drawstring-waist slacks and red canvas deck shoes. He'd knotted a yellow kerchief around his right knee—for no particular reason that she could tell. He looked wonderful. Exactly as she remembered him—except, perhaps, for the small lines around his eyes. They seemed deeper, more prominent than they'd appeared before, making him look almost his age. "What are you doing here, Clay?"

"I need my eyes checked," he replied casually, leaning back in the chair and examining the equipment around him with interest. "Do you really know how to use all this stuff?"

"You came all the way from San Francisco to have your eyes examined?" Spring repeated sceptically, ignoring his question.

"Only the best for these baby blues," he replied, batting his eyelashes at her audaciously.

"Your eyes are not baby blue, they're somewhere between blue and green." Spring twisted her hands in front of her, her heart pounding beneath the wrinkled white lab coat. She was fighting two impulses, both equally inappropriate. The first was to run screaming from the room, protecting herself from any further pain at this man's hands. The second was to throw herself on his colorfully clad body and ravish him, keeping him chained to the chair until she grew tired of him. She figured that fifty or sixty years ought to do it.

"So you went to optometry college in Memphis?" Clay asked, reading the diploma on the wall.

"Yes. Clay—"

"See, I read that. No problem, right?"

Spring moistened her lips, still staring at him from the spot that she seemed to have been frozen to. She wouldn't ask him again why he was here, she decided. Her voice seemed to have left her, anyway.

Clay looked at her, smiled and held out his hand. "Come here."

It took her a second to propel herself across the room. And then she was in his lap and his arms were around her and he was kissing her. There were tears on her face, tears on his, and they were both apologizing between kisses.

"Spring, I'm so sorry."

"Oh, Clay, I never should have said—"

"God, I've missed you."

"I've missed you, too. And you *do* have dignity."

"And I'm sorry I called you a snob. You're—"

Spring leaned backward, frowning. "You didn't call me a snob."

"I didn't?"

"No."

"Oh." He kissed her again, then smiled. "Then I'm sorry I thought about calling you a snob."

She cupped his face in her hands and stared fiercely into his eyes. "Clay, *why* are you here?"

"To get my eyes checked, Spring. And to see you."

She laughed, happier than she'd been in four long months. "You really want me to examine your eyes?"

"You bet. You can handle it, can't you?"

"I can handle it." She leaned forward and planted her mouth firmly on his, her arms going around his neck.

"Dr. Reed, there's a tele— Oh, excuse me."

Flushing vividly, Spring looked around to find her assistant staring at her in wide-eyed astonishment. "Oh, Andi. What is it?"

"You have a telephone call."

Feeling Clay vibrating with suppressed laughter beneath her, Spring planted her hands on his chest and pushed herself out of his lap. "All right, I'll take it. And then," she added to Clay, "I'm going to test your vision. Actually, I've been wanting to do so ever since I caught you playing slide trombone with the play program on our first date."

Clay frowned. "You're not really planning to put me in glasses, are you?"

"We'll see," she replied mysteriously, throwing him a laughing glance over her shoulder as she left the room. She decided to take the call in the business office that looked out on the empty reception area.

"Want me to go keep our patient happy while you take this call?" Kelsey asked hopefully when Spring reached for the phone on Kelsey's desk.

Spring held the receiver, her finger hovering over the hold button. Now she knew why she'd chosen to use this particular telephone. "Did you really give him your phone number?"

"You bet. Isn't he gorgeous?"

Spring leaned her hip on Kelsey's desk and gave her friend a hard stare. "I want your phone number changed. Immediately."

With a sputter of startled laughter Kelsey dropped her pencil and stared back at Spring. "Does this mean you're over that Clay guy in California?"

"This means he *is* that Clay guy. And he's not in California, he's in my examining room!"

Kelsey's mouth fell open comically. "That's him? No kidding?" At Spring's happy nod she sighed gustily. "Wouldn't you know it. I fall in love at first sight, and the guy's already taken. Besides that, I think I've just lost your grandmother's earrings!"

Her heart jumping, Spring took a deep breath and took her call, trying to sound professional when all she wanted to do was sing with joy.

Clay had come for her!

10

"SPRING, ARE YOU quite sure I need glasses?"

"Clay, I've told you that they're only for reading. You'll be much more comfortable with your school paperwork when your eyes are under less strain."

"What did you call what I have again?"

Spring smiled indulgently and unlocked the door to her apartment. "Hyperopia. You're slightly farsighted, Clay, and you have a touch of astigmatism. I explained all that in my office." She pushed open the door and stepped in, her stomach tightening nervously now that she and Clay were actually going to be alone for the first time in four months.

"Yes, I know, but . . . glasses! Just think how everyone will tease me."

He reminded her of Danny ready to beat up Bobby Clary for calling him "Four Eyes." She had to laugh. "They certainly would tease you if I'd let you choose those frames you tried on. Honestly, Clay, they made you look like . . . like Elton John, in one of his flashier concert outfits."

"Hey, you're the one who carries them in stock."

"Yes, but I never sell them to adults. Only to very strange teenagers."

"And I qualify on only one of those counts, right?" Clay walked around the living room into which she'd led him, trailing his fingers along a particularly nice

Louis Philippe reproduction table. "You seem to be very good at your job. Very thorough."

"The exam doesn't normally take quite that long. But then, most of my patients don't pull me onto their laps or pinch me in various places when I look into their eyes."

He grinned. "I have to admit that I haven't enjoyed an examination so much in a long time." Without waiting for her response he looked once more around what he could see of her apartment. "This is nice. Very nice."

Pleased, she smiled at him. "Somehow I thought you'd like it."

"Odd, isn't it? This could almost be my place." He shot her a look that made her skin tingle, then glanced at the painting above her mantel. "I was with Summer when she bought this. She said you'd seen it and liked it."

"Yes." She didn't tell him why she hadn't bought it for herself. Nor did she tell him how many times in the past weeks she'd stared at it and cried. "I haven't thanked you yet for the bracelet."

"Yes, you did. You sent me a very proper little note thanking me and telling me that I shouldn't have sent it." A note he hadn't answered. Stopping beside her, he caught her hand in his and lifted it, admiring the bracelet on her wrist. "Thank you for not sending it back. I wanted you to have it."

"Why?" she asked, the word a mere whisper.

He pressed a kiss into her palm. "I wanted you to wear it and think of me."

She swallowed. "I didn't need a bracelet for that."

"Did you think of me, sweet Spring?" He pulled her closer, his hands sliding around her waist as he asked the question.

"Yes," she murmured through suddenly dry lips.

"A lot?"

"Yes."

"Good," he muttered into her hair. "Because I haven't stopped thinking of you since you left. Or missing you. Or wanting you."

"Oh, Clay." She didn't consciously place her arms around his neck, but suddenly they were there, and she was crowding close to him with all the hunger that had built up in the months since she'd seen him. He groaned and gathered her into his arms, holding her as if he'd never let her go again. She prayed that he wouldn't.

"Spring, there's so much I want to say to you, but all I can think about right now is making love to you. God, it's been so long."

"Yes, Clay, please. We can talk later." Trembling in anticipation, she pressed dozens of little kisses on his jaw, his neck, his cheek, anywhere she could reach.

His hand removed her glasses and placed them on a nearby table, then went to her hair, scattering pins across her cream-colored carpet. "You're wearing it up again," he complained.

"There's been no one to wear it down for," she answered, shaking her head slowly so that the tresses he'd loosened fell in a tumble around her shoulders.

"Thank God." He lifted her into his arms, swinging her in a full circle before stopping to kiss her. "Where's your bedroom?" he demanded when he released her mouth.

"Upstairs, first door on the left," she answered, snuggling into his shoulder.

"Too far." He lowered her to the carpet, following immediately to capture her mouth again. Before the kiss ended, he had her plum cotton shirtdress unbuttoned and halfway off. She cooperated eagerly, as anxious as he to be rid of the barriers between them. When her clothing was gone, they both began on his, tossing the colorful garments into a careless heap beside them. "Come here," he muttered, when nothing was left to separate them.

He pulled her into his arms, then rolled so that she was stretched on top of him, her hair falling around their faces. "This is what I've needed for the past four months," he told her, his fingers sliding slowly down her back to cup her bottom and hold her to him. "Nothing between us. No miles, no arguments, no clothing. Just you and me."

She lowered her head to nibble on his lower lip, wriggling a little to settle herself more comfortably against him. He was hard and hot against her, eliciting a warm, throbbing response from deep within her. "What took you so long to get here?" she asked, amazed at the sultry sensuality of her own voice. She was so different with Clay. Sexy and uninhibited and playful. She loved the way he made her feel. She loved him, but she wasn't ready to tell him. Not until he gave her some indication of his own feelings.

God, he loved her. He pulled her mouth firmly to his, kissing her as if to make up for four months of deprivation. She felt so good on top of him. Holding her, he twisted onto his side. She felt so good beside him. He rolled again. She felt so good beneath him.

"You feel good everywhere," he told her huskily, relishing the little laugh he received in response. "Am I too heavy for you?"

"No," she answered, looking up at him with an adoring expression that made him want to shout in masculine triumph. Or cry. He kissed her instead.

"Love me, Clay. Please love me."

"I will, Spring. I do. I love you so much." And then he was moving, slipping inside her to lose himself in the dark velvet depths of her, and she was curling around him to hold him and he thought he'd never felt such pleasure in his entire life. Or at least, he amended on one last, rational fragment of thought, not since the last time he'd been inside her.

Then he couldn't think at all but could only close his eyes and let instinct drive him, shuddering as she lifted to meet each deep, desperate thrust. He'd wanted to take it slowly this first time after their separation, to savor each moment, but his needs had flared out of his control. He struggled fiercely to ensure that Spring found her own pleasure before he gave in to the need for release, deeply satisfied when she convulsed beneath him, crying out brokenly. Only then did he let go, her name leaving his lips in a gasp as he went rigid for a long, pulsing moment, then collapsed heavily on top of her.

Almost immediately he rolled to his side to relieve her of his weight. But he refused to let her go. He'd never willingly let her go again.

Spring took a deep breath and then another, willing her heartbeat to slow, her thoughts to clear. She found it almost hard to believe that she was lying on her living-room floor, that it was a Monday evening after a fairly typical day at her office. All comprehension of time and place had left her while Clay had made love with her, and now she was forced to entirely reorient herself. She hadn't really been to paradise.

Or had she? Had Clay really told her he loved her?

She wrapped her arms around him and held him tightly. "I can't believe you're actually here. I'm afraid I'll wake up and you'll be gone again."

"No, sweetheart. I'm here. I can't believe I stayed away so long."

She wanted to ask why he had, but she didn't know if she was ready yet to spoil the mood by bringing up that stupid fight they'd had. Instead, she toyed lazily with one of the few golden curls scattered across his chest and asked, "Why did you tell Andi and Kelsey that your name was Mr. Crowe?"

He chuckled, his hand moving in idle patterns on her shoulder. "I thought you'd figure that out. Crow is the entrée on my menu for tonight's dinner." He sobered abruptly. "I'm sorry, Spring. For everything that happened between us that last night in California. I was spoiling for a fight when I saw you that night, and I all but leaped on the first difference of opinion that came up."

"All right, I accept your apology. And I'm sorry, too."

He shook his head against the carpet, then pushed himself upright, helping her up to sit beside him, her long legs tucked beside her. "No, Spring. Don't just shrug it off. We need to talk about it so you'll understand what happened."

She sighed. "I guess you're right. I just hate to bring it up now, after everything has been so nice."

"We're not going to argue again. I promise. I just want to explain."

She reached for her blouse. "All right. I suppose it *is* time for us to talk. Past time."

He reached out to still her hand. "What are you doing?"

"I'm getting dressed."

"No, don't. You're beautiful exactly the way you are."

She flushed, squirming a bit under his lambent regard. "I feel strange sitting here without any clothes on."

"You'll get used to it." He grinned, deliberately distracting her from her modest self-consciousness. "Surely you're not still accusing me of being dressed funny? This time my ego really *would* be hurt."

She laughed, as he'd intended, and shook her head. "You are a beautiful man, Clay McEntire. A perfect specimen. Well, almost perfect. There's that scar on your stomach. But even that looks good on you. What caused it?" she asked because she was genuinely curious about the thin white line that was a bit too crooked to be caused by a surgeon's blade and because she was still trying to delay their talk about the quarrel.

"A switchblade," he answered calmly, and somehow she knew that the talk had already begun.

"You were knifed?" she whispered in horror. "By one of your kids?"

He shook his head. "In a fight, when I was sixteen. I was carrying a knife, too, Spring. I just wasn't as good with mine as the other guy was with his."

"Oh, Clay." She reached out to touch his cheek. He was so beautiful, so wholesome and happy looking that she tended to forget the darker side of his past.

He caught her hand in his, kissed it, then lowered it to his bare thigh. "I've told you about my past, Spring. It wasn't so nice. My parents were cold, demanding people, and I could never live up to their expectations. Appearances meant everything to them and very little to me. I wanted so much to love them, as every child wants to love his parents, but their continuous emotional rejection made me angry. I took my rage out on them and everyone else around me, even myself. And that's why I was mad at you that night in California."

"But, Clay, I hadn't rejected you," she protested, her forehead creasing with a frown as she tried to understand. "Just the opposite, in fact. We'd made love."

He captured her other hand, leaning forward as he gripped her fingers in his. "Don't you see, sweetheart? I was anticipating your rejection. I was angry with you before the fact because I was so certain it was going to happen. Stupid, I know, but don't forget that I'd had several years of experience with rejection and it's not always easy to put the past behind me. You kept talking about returning home, and I knew how much it would hurt me when you left, so I took the initiative, I guess, and hurt you before you could hurt me."

"You were so angry with me for agreeing with Tony's parents."

"Another scar from the past," he confessed. "I was dragged home by the cops a couple of times when I'd had enough and decided to leave. It's a humiliating and pride-destroying experience, especially if you get a couple of thick-skulled cops who couldn't care less about kids and get their kicks by treating them like dirt. I work very closely with the police at times now, and I've developed a great deal of respect for most of them, but I'll never forget how it felt."

"And that's why you identified so closely with Tony."

"Yes. But you were entitled to your opinion, Spring. I could have told you how I felt and why, instead of shouting at you for expressing your own thoughts. I'm sorry."

"I was scared, too, Clay," she admitted quietly, her eyes dropping to their clasped hands. "You seemed so happy with your life, and I didn't think I fit in. I'm not adventurous and impulsive and outgoing, like Summer and your other friends. And I'm not exotic and beautiful, like the women in your past. I was becoming so deeply involved with you, but I thought you only wanted a fling with me because of a fleeting attraction. Your odd behavior the night we quarreled only seemed to confirm that suspicion."

Clay sighed deeply and raised her hands to his mouth, pressing his lips to her knuckles before lowering them again. "My beautiful, fascinating Spring. *Why* are you so determined to put yourself down? What makes you think that you're so uninteresting, and what will it take for me to convince you that you're dead wrong?"

She shrugged a little, embarrassed. "I guess my behavior is shaped by my past, just like yours. I'm so used to being compared to my extroverted, exuberant younger sisters. When we were little, Summer was always clowning around, performing, making people laugh with her impersonations and her songs and dances. And Autumn was a scrapper, a beautiful redheaded tomboy who impressed everyone with her fiery personality and her athletic prowess. I was known as the quiet one, the studious one, the shy one. My mother was always talking about the mischief Summer and Autumn got into, telling her friends the latest thing one or the other had done, like she was complaining but secretly amused by them. When she mentioned me, it was only to say what a good girl I was.

"I'm not saying she didn't love me as much as she loved my sisters," she added hastily. "I'm sure she did. And she was—*is* very proud of me. But I just got used to being on the sidelines, unable to compete for attention the way my sisters did. It wasn't bad. I liked being out of the limelight. I wasn't comfortable with too much attention."

"Poor love," Clay crooned, smiling tenderly at her. "It must have been as hard for you to always live up to the label of good girl as it was for me to live up to the label of bad boy."

She smiled faintly and bit her lip. "Oh, I used to rebel sometimes, in my own quiet, unobtrusive ways. I'd play practical jokes and never tell anyone who did them. People used to blame them on Summer and Autumn and think it was all hilariously funny. Or I'd unexpectedly accept a dare when no one thought I would. I broke my arm once climbing a tree that everyone knew was rotten, just because Tommy Trenton dared me to. My family was shocked, but I was secretly quite proud of that cast."

"Just like I dared you to dress funky the night we went to the play at my school," he remembered with an appreciative grin.

"Mmm. And I've lived the life of a modern single woman since I left home," she added thoughtfully. "There haven't been many men in my life, but I doubt that my mother would have approved of all my actions. She's probably quite convinced that Autumn and I are still virgins simply because we're not married yet and that Summer was an innocent bride. She's very old-fashioned in that way."

Clay chuckled. "You don't think you're underestimating your mother a bit?"

"Oh, no." Spring laughed softly and shook her head. "No matter what she might suspect, she'd never admit it, even to herself. She prefers blissful ignorance—like all mothers, I suppose."

"You'll probably be the same way with our . . . with your children." Clay stumbled over the Freudian slip, then sobered immediately. "About the future, Spring . . ."

Still dazed by the thought of having children with him, Spring tensed, a bit nervous about what he was going to say. "What . . . what about it?"

"Let's delay it awhile, shall we? What we have together is still so new, so wonderfully mind-boggling, that I'd like to savor it before we move on to the next step. We have a lot of decisions to make, a lot to discuss, and I fully intend to do so soon, but how about if we take a couple of weeks just to get to know each other better?"

That sounded fine to her—on one condition. "Are you staying here during those couple of weeks?"

"If you'll have me," he replied with a winsome smile. "I'm taking a vacation. It's my turn."

"I'll have you," she told him, a bit too fervently, she thought immediately. She backtracked a little. "I can't take off work, though. My appointment calendar's full, and I can't take off again so soon."

"That's okay. I didn't expect you to."

"What will you do with yourself during working hours?" she asked, concerned that he would be bored.

"I could stand around your office and watch you work," he suggested teasingly. "No? In that case, I'll play tourist. I've never been to Arkansas. Maybe I'll find some barefoot hillbillies, if I look hard enough."

Spring scowled ferociously at him. "Are you daring to insult my state?"

He released her hands to hold both of his up, palm outward, in a gesture of conciliation. "Of course not! I was only teasing."

"Good. You just might be surprised at what you find in Arkansas," she told him smugly.

"I've already found something in Arkansas that's the best thing I've ever discovered. You."

She melted. "Thank you."

"This time together will also give you a chance to see what it's like to live with me," Clay pointed out, only half-teasingly. "I'm not your most normal guy, you know. And I do tend to get moody occasionally. Not very often, you understand. But I don't leave my dirty socks lying around," he added with a bit of boyish boasting.

"You don't wear socks, Clay," Spring informed him sweetly.

"That's right, I don't." He looked abashed for a moment, then grinned. "Maybe I should buy some and not leave them lying around."

"I don't think that will be necessary. I'm sure we can find another virtue in you if we look hard enough."

He seemed to consider that for a moment, then shot her a challenging look. "You're too far away. If you're going to find a virtue in me, you're going to have to look closely."

"Is that right?" Her brow lifted at the dare, as he'd known it would. "You know, the light in here is a bit dim. There's a better light in the bathroom."

He looked intrigued. "The bathroom?"

"Mmm. I thought I'd take a shower. I worked up quite a sweat today—at work," she added saucily. Then, remembering another challenge he'd once made her, she tilted her head and looked at him through her lashes. "I'd be happy to wash your back, Clay."

He, too, remembered telling her that one day she would offer to wash his back. His eyes gleamed with pleasure as he stood and held out his hand to her. "Only if you'll allow me to return the favor."

"I think that can be arranged."

The shower took a very long time. The water had run quite cold by the time it finally ended. By then they had soaped each other from head to toe, Spring had discovered two more tiny scars on Clay's body, and he'd gleefully located a shallow, round, nine-month-old chicken-pox scar on her left breast, just to the side of her turgid pink nipple. Twisting the chilly water off, he covered the small imperfection with his mouth, which led to a painstaking exploration of the rest of her body, supposedly to find other reminders of the childhood disease she'd contracted so recently. He didn't find any, but by the time he'd concluded his search, neither of them remembered what he'd been looking for.

After they'd languorously dried each other with huge, fluffy towels, Spring took Clay's hand and led him into her bedroom, reminding him that she was supposed to be looking for his virtues. With a boldness that was new to her—and delightful to him—she made love to him. Slowly. Thoroughly. Imaginatively. He loved every minute of it, and he managed to tell her so in broken gasps and strangled groans.

Afterward they both fell asleep, exhausted but deeply content. They hadn't eaten dinner, but they'd satisfied their hunger in other ways. Sometime during the night they raided the refrigerator for sandwiches, then made love again. Clay went back to sleep almost immediately. Spring lay awake for a short time, wondering about the future they'd been reluctant to discuss, but then she decided to adopt Clay's live-for-the-moment attitude and she, too, fell asleep, cradled close in his arms.

SO THAT CLAY COULD USE her car, Spring called Kelsey the next morning and asked for a ride. She left for work with her hair a bit mussed, her lips slightly swollen, and with just barely enough time to get to her office before her first appointment. But her violet eyes sparkled with love, her cheeks glowed with happiness and she couldn't seem to stop smiling. If she still worried about the future, she managed to hide it—even from herself. She was in love, and Clay was here, and she intended to relish every moment.

"I would say that you had a very...interesting night," Kelsey commented after taking one look at her friend's face.

Blushing rosily, Spring straightened her breeze-tossed hair, which she'd left down that morning. "It was... nice."

"Nice." Kelsey sounded a lot like Summer when she repeated the word with disdain. "Sure."

"Okay, it was fabulous. What do you want, play-by-play reporting?"

Grinning, Kelsey nodded avidly.

Spring laughed and shook her head. "Forget it. I wouldn't have time, anyway. Mr. Abernathy is due at the office in less than fifteen minutes."

"Hey, you're the one who was five minutes late coming down to the parking lot."

Spring blushed again. "I know."

"Did he ask you to marry him?"

"Mr. Abernathy?" Spring inquired, being deliberately obtuse.

Kelsey sighed gustily. "No. Clay Crowe McEntire. Did he ask you?"

"No, Kelsey."

"Did he tell you that he loves you?"

Spring hesitated, then shrugged. "In a way."

"In a way? What's that supposed to mean?"

"Kelsey, really. I don't have time for this, and I'm not sure that I'd want to go into it if I did. It's awfully personal."

Kelsey smiled ruefully and nodded her dark head. "I know. It's just that I can't help worrying about you a little. I can't forget the way you looked on your birthday when you opened that gift from him. You were so devastated. This man has such power to hurt you."

Spring moistened her lips and tucked a strand of hair behind the earpiece of her glasses. "Kelsey, I know you're only concerned because you care about me, but I really don't want to talk about this just now, okay? Clay and I agreed to spend some time together before we discuss the future, and I think it was a good idea. I don't want to rush into anything at this point, nor do I want to spoil my enjoyment of being with him by worrying about what may or may not happen."

"I understand," Kelsey told her, though her dark eyes were still concerned. "Be happy, Spring. You deserve it." She parked the car in her parking space, then hesitated and turned to her friend, smiling as if she were worried that she might have put a damper on Spring's good spirits. "By the way, if you get tired of having the guy around, I'd be willing to put up with him for a few hours."

Spring laughed. "I'll just bet you would. Sorry, Kel, no chance. I'm hanging on to this one."

"I don't blame you."

"Thanks for the concern, Kelsey," Spring added quickly before climbing out of the small car. She was anxious to stay busy, knowing that the time until she

was with Clay again would pass too slowly if she gave
herself a chance to think about it.

She'd half expected Clay to call her sometime during
the day, but he didn't. Nor did he show up at lunch-
time. She wondered what he was doing with himself.
She wondered if he'd like what he saw of her home
state. And, finally, she wondered what was going to
happen between them. It seemed that no amount of
determination on her part could stop her from worrying about the future when she found herself with half
an hour between appointments late that afternoon, due
to a last-minute cancellation. She loved her city, her
state and the practice she'd built, but she loved Clay so
much more. If he asked—as she suspected that he
would—could she leave the rest behind for him?

It wouldn't be easy, starting over. It scared her witless to think about it. Maybe she'd be content just to be
Clay's wife—assuming he asked her to marry him, she
added hastily, staring sightlessly at a patient's file. She
could keep his home for him, have his children, wait
patiently in his lovely house until he finished with his
job and his volunteer work. It wouldn't be so bad.

It would be awful. She'd worked so hard for her degree. She loved her work. She'd go crazy with nothing
to do but clean house and cook meals. Even if she had
children, they would start school eventually, and then
where would she be? Perhaps she would choose to take
off a couple of years if she had a baby, but the opera-
tive word was "choose." She didn't like the idea of giving up her career just because she was afraid to start
over in a new place.

No, she told herself bravely, she wouldn't give up her
work. If Clay wanted her to go back with him to San
Francisco, she'd do it, but she'd have to find a job there

in her field. Perhaps she couldn't start her own practice again immediately, but maybe she could enter a partnership in an existing clinic. It wasn't that she didn't like San Francisco. She did. She thought it was a beautiful city. But, oh, how she'd miss Arkansas.

She wouldn't miss it nearly as much as she'd missed Clay during the past four months, she reminded herself. She couldn't even bring herself to consider how she would feel if she was separated from him now, after being given another glimpse of happiness with him. Even the thought was painful enough to cause her to flinch.

She quickly busied herself with work, pulling her thoughts away from the future, unwilling to dwell on the uncertainties just then.

"I MISSED YOU."

"I missed you, too. What did you do with yourself today?" Spring asked, her voice rather muffled since her head was buried deep within Clay's shoulder.

"I looked around, checked out Little Rock." He held her slightly away from him, giving her a proud-of-himself smile. "Did you know that this city has a symphony orchestra, two opera companies, a couple of community theaters, a ballet company, some very nice golf courses, hundreds of acres of beautiful parks, a zoo, a—"

"Clay, I know all that!" She laughed and clapped her hand over his mouth. "I've lived in this area all my life. Why are you telling me about it?"

"Just showing off what I've learned today," he informed her after removing her hand. "It's a fascinating town. The chamber of commerce was happy to give me all kinds of information."

"You visited the chamber of commerce?"

"Sure. It's the best place to start when you're learning a new city."

Why was he going to so much trouble to learn about Little Rock? The question puzzled her until his lips distracted her by making a little trail down her throat toward the open neck of her summery dress. "What are you doing, Clay?"

"Can't you guess?" He unfastened one button, his lips following the downward path of his fingers.

"What about dinner?"

"I can wait awhile. How about you?"

She closed her eyes and moaned softly when he found her breasts with fingers and lips. "I'm getting hungrier—but not for dinner."

He laughed softly and caught her up in his arms. "We may both lose weight during these next few weeks."

"So we'll be fashionably thin," she replied, smiling as she put her arms around his neck.

"You don't need to lose any weight," he murmured, his long strides carrying them quickly to her bedroom. "I promise to feed you well tonight. Later."

"Yes." She reached upward for his kiss as he lowered her to the bed. "Much later."

11

"AHEM."

"Just a minute, sweetheart, let me finish this article. It's about a psychologist here in town who has an interesting new method for treating emotionally disturbed teenagers." Clay held the paper a bit farther away from him, focusing with interest on the article that had grabbed his attention.

Spring sighed and walked up to his chair, sliding his stylish new glasses onto his nose. "*Now* you can finish your article," she informed him, then turned and went back to her own chair, where she'd been reading a professional journal when she noticed that Clay wasn't wearing his glasses. She'd gotten them for him on Wednesday morning and it was now Thursday evening, and he was still having trouble remembering to wear them when he read.

Clay gave her a sheepish grin, then went back to his article, swinging his leg over the arm of the easy chair in which he'd sprawled—the chair he'd claimed as his own during the four days since his arrival in Little Rock. Spring ignored the journal in her lap to admire her lover for a moment. His hair was mussed, he was barefoot, he was wearing a vivid green polo shirt with blue-purple-and-jade madras-plaid cuffed pants, and he wore her cat draped around his neck like a muffler. He looked wonderful. The glasses, with their thin metal frames, were very attractive on him. She couldn't tear her gaze away from him.

She had never been happier in her life. She'd always thought it would be difficult for her to adjust to living with someone after being on her own for so long, but she loved living with Clay. They were completely compatible, in bed and out, and she couldn't bear the thought of living without him now. In four days he had implanted himself so firmly in her life and her heart that she knew he had become a vital part of her.

He was still spending his days, as far as she knew, roaming the local area, exploring anything that caught his interest. In the evenings he took her with him, showing her parts of the city that she'd never seen, even as long as she'd lived there. Only the night before they had taken a ride on a paddleboat down the Arkansas River, which ran right alongside downtown Little Rock. He was impressed by Little Rock's cosmopolitan development and the small-town atmosphere that somehow remained. He was amused by the fanatic loyalty to the University of Arkansas football team, the Razorbacks, as evidenced by the snorting red hogs depicted on signs, bumper stickers, clothing, household articles, billboards—just about everywhere he looked, he'd informed Spring.

"And this is summertime," she'd told him with a laugh. "You should see us during football season!" And then she'd fallen silent, wondering where he—where *they*—would be come fall. She only hoped that, wherever they were, they'd be together.

Clay had expressed an avid interest in seeing other parts of the state, naming off several places he'd like to see and things he wanted to do. Spring had accused him of being a compulsive tourist, but she'd made a reservation at a popular lakeside hotel in nearby Hot Springs National Park for the weekend, eager to show him as much as she could of her state while she had the chance. She was delighted by his complimentary attitude and hoped he wasn't just saying what he thought she wanted to hear. They'd decided to wait until the following weekend to visit her family in Rose Bud, though neither would admit aloud that they didn't want to spend time with her family until their future was somewhat more settled.

"You know, I think I'll give this guy a call next week," Clay mused, breaking in on Spring's thoughts as he looked up from his newspaper to find her gaze on him. "I'd like to meet him and discuss his new treatment method. It sounds interesting."

Spring smiled, knowing that Clay would probably be fast friends with the other man by the end of their meeting. He seemed to have a talent for making friends. Her neighbor, Mr. English, a man old enough to be Clay's father, had already become a friend, just from a chance meeting outside the apartments, and Clay had promised to go fishing with the other man one afternoon during the next week.

The telephone rang and Spring got up to answer it. Clay followed her into the kitchen and poured himself a soft drink while she talked to Kelsey. Spring looked up at him. "Kelsey wants to know if we're interested in a pool party-cookout tomorrow at six. A friend of ours has just decided he wants to have a party at his house tomorrow."

"Sounds like fun. Come to think of it, I've never seen you in a bathing suit." He gave her a teasing leer, his eyebrows wiggling. "Or Kelsey," he added thoughtfully, earning himself a punch on the arm. "Hey! You almost made me spill my Coke!"

"Clay likes the idea," Spring reported to her friend on the phone. "And, Kelsey, wear your navy-blue swimsuit, will you? You know, the one with the turtleneck and the patch on the right knee." When she hung up, Kelsey was still laughing.

Spring extended one hand in Clay's direction, trying to hold on to a fierce scowl. "Okay, buster, hand it over."

"Hand what over? My drink?"

"No, Kelsey's phone number. I forgot about it until now."

Clay laughed and shook his head. "Sorry, don't have it."

"She said she gave it to you." She knew her eyes were dancing with laughter, but she managed not to grin as she teased him. "Give."

"I really don't have it," he insisted humorously. "I tossed it in the wastebasket in your examining room when Andi ushered me in."

"You did?"

"Yep. I didn't know she was your best friend, but I knew I wasn't interested in any other woman's phone number. There hasn't been another woman for me since I looked up one Friday evening in March and saw a beautiful blonde standing in a doorway looking down her nose at my clothing."

Spring gave in to her smile and looped her arms around his neck. "Good. You just passed one test."

"I didn't know I was being tested." He set his soft drink down on the table, out of danger, and crossed his arms around her waist.

"Women always test men, didn't you know that?"

"How am I doing?"

"You did very well on the one about leaving your dirty socks lying around. You don't squeeze your toothpaste from the middle, you don't snore, you pick up after yourself and you don't keep other women's phone numbers—that's a big one, by the way."

Clay smiled smugly, dropping a kiss on the end of her nose. "Darn near perfect, aren't I?"

"Oh, you have a few flaws," she retorted, not wanting all that praise to go to his already swelling head.

"Such as?"

"You forget to wear your new glasses."

"I'll work on that one."

"And you get the newspaper all out of order before I read it."

"Oh. Sorry."

"You're a terrible cook."

"I suppose I could learn."

"And you've stolen my cat's affections. Missy thinks you're the greatest thing since catnip."

"And what do *you* think?"

"I think you're the greatest thing since catnip."

He grinned and dropped his head to kiss her, laughing when they bumped glasses. "I can tell that this is going to take practice."

Her own smile faded a bit as she fought to keep from telling him that she was willing to practice for a lifetime. He still hadn't brought up their future, and she wouldn't be the one to break their agreement, even though the subject had been weighing more heavily on her mind with each passing day. "We could take them off," she offered instead.

"Among other things," he added, tugging suggestively at the collar of her knit top.

"Yes," she agreed. She wanted to tell him she loved him, she thought wistfully as they walked side by side to the bedroom. She need to tell him. But that subject, too, was one that hadn't come up since Monday, when Clay had told her he loved her in a surge of passion. He hadn't told her since then, and she wasn't sure why. Was it because he wasn't sure himself? If so, she wouldn't pressure him by telling him her own feelings.

But, oh, how she loved him.

"THAT MAN OF YOURS is beautiful enough to make a grown woman weep, Spring," Kelsey said with a deep sigh, her eyes trained on Clay as he piled a plate high with a steaming grilled hamburger, pickles and chips. In his tropical-print surfing shorts that he'd chosen to wear with striped suspenders and a red sleeveless T-shirt, Clay wouldn't have been hard to spot in the crowd even if he hadn't been so tall and so very handsome. The early-evening sun, still bright and hot at this time of day in July, glinted off his hair, turning it to pure gold.

"Yes, I know," Spring agreed complacently, loving the proprietary feeling Kelsey's words had given her. Sitting cross-legged on a blanket, she took a big bite of her own burger—Clay was on his second—and watched him as he talked with a heavyset man in the line beside him. Gordon, the man Clay was talking to, owned the sprawling ranch-style house on fifty acres only a ten-minute drive out of Little Rock and frequently hosted these impromptu parties. Self-employed, he was able both financially and timewise to do so. Kelsey had met him just after she'd moved to Little Rock, and she was responsible for bringing Spring into Gordon's huge, heterogeneous circle. Clay had wasted no time getting acquainted with Spring's friends, mixing in as if he'd known everyone for years.

"And he's such a snappy dresser," Kelsey added with a grin.

Spring choked on her dinner and giggled.

"Something tells me you're laughing at me again," Clay complained as he joined them on the blanket, slipping off his red huaraches to tuck his bare feet under him. He winked at Kelsey as he looped a lazy arm around Spring's neck and hugged her. "She's got this crazy idea that I have strange taste in clothing," he explained.

Kelsey widened her eyes dramatically. "No! Why would she think that?"

"Beats me." Clay released Spring to attack his second hamburger as Kelsey's date, Wade, rejoined them after having fetched another mug of draft beer for himself and Kelsey.

"Thanks, Wade." Kelsey smiled at the solidly built ex-Razorback-turned-insurance salesman, then turned her attention back to Clay. "Spring told me that the two of you are leaving for Hot Springs in the morning. You'll like it. It's a beautiful area. Be sure and go up in the new observation tower on Hot Springs Mountain. It's over two hundred feet tall, and you can see the Ouachita Mountains and Lake Ouachita and Hamilton Lake and all of Hot Springs. It's gorgeous. Oh, and don't forget the Mid-America Museum and the Wax Museum and..."

Seeing that Clay was following Kelsey's every word with avid interest, Spring laughed and interrupted. "Kelsey, give us a break. We're only going to be there Saturday and Sunday, and Clay's already a compulsive tourist. Believe me, if it's there, he'll find it."

Clay only grinned and popped another chip into his mouth.

Half an hour later Clay and Kelsey and Wade were working off calories in a Hacky Sack circle while Spring, who'd never mastered that particular game, watched and laughed at them. Her eyes lingered on Clay as he adroitly fielded the small, leather-covered foot bag with his knee, then kicked it with the side of his foot to Wade, who expertly bounced the little ball off his own knee to Kelsey.

"Hello, Spring. You're looking very well," a familiar male voice said from behind her.

She turned her head to smile at the attractive man with neatly trimmed brown hair and rather serious green eyes, finding herself thinking in some amusement that his sharply creased jeans and Izod knit shirt looked atypically casual. "Hello, Roger. When did you get here?"

"Just a few minutes ago." He leaned down a bit awkwardly to kiss her cheek. "How pretty you look." Spring had worn a peacock-blue romper, brighter than her usual pastels, with white sandals. She'd left her hair down to tumble in loose curls at her shoulders and had stowed her glasses in their case in her purse. She knew she looked more relaxed and casual than Roger was accustomed to seeing her. Probably happier, too.

"Thank you, Roger." Come to think of it, Roger had a new glow in his own eyes. "Are you here with someone?"

His smile was just a bit shy—something else new for him. "Yes." He nodded toward a young woman engaged in a laughing conversation with Gordon. "Her name is Cathy Fleetwood. We're, uh, we're engaged."

Her eyes widening in surprise, Spring examined Roger's fiancée more closely. The tall, slender woman was strikingly attractive—and cheerfully flamboyant. In her mid-twenties, she wore her golden-brown hair in thick, wavy layers to her shoulders. Her huge blue eyes were dramatically highlighted with makeup, she wore enormous earrings that swayed with each movement of her head and her summer gauze jumpsuit was striped in hot pink, turquoise and blinding white. She looked like a feminine version of Clay. Summer couldn't help laughing, then quickly explained when Roger looked offended. "I'm just happy for you. She looks very nice."

He relaxed only marginally, still uncertain why she had laughed. "Thank you. I am happy. We're going to be married next month."

An obviously possessive arm went around Spring's waist and Clay loomed over her. "Did you miss me, sweetheart?"

"Of course I did, Clay." She smiled indulgently up at him, realizing that he must have seen Roger kiss her cheek. And he wasn't too happy about it. "Clay McEntire, this is Roger Nichols."

Recognizing Roger's name, Clay scowled for just a moment before holding out his hand.

Roger shook the proffered hand warmly, casting a glance at Clay's clothing before turning a ruefully amused look on Spring. Now he knew why she'd laughed, she realized. Both she and Roger had fallen in love with people diametrically different from themselves, and they knew it. No wonder they hadn't been able to hold on to their own relationship. Neither of them had been what the other needed. She smiled brilliantly at her former lover, silently wishing him happiness. His eyes returned the blessing before he walked away to join his fiancée and their host.

"Just what was that all about?" Clay demanded, bristling with masculine aggressiveness.

"What?"

"That look you gave each other. I thought you said everything was over between you and Roger."

"It is. Completely over." She turned in his arms, locking her hands behind his back and smiling up at him. "Clay, are you actually jealous?"

"Yes," he answered, looking stricken. "Dammit, Spring, I've never been jealous in my life!"

"Don't be, Clay. Roger's engaged and very happily so. And even if he weren't, you wouldn't have to worry. Don't you know how much I—" Her smile faded as she stopped herself, then she lifted her chin and finished the sentence. "Don't you know how much I love you, Clay McEntire?"

There. She had said it. She was tired of hiding her feelings.

"And I love you," Clay whispered, lowering his head to hers. "Oh, God, how I love you!" And forgetting that they were not alone—or, more likely, not caring that they had an audience—he kissed her with all the love and need inside him.

Too happy to be embarrassed, Spring returned the kiss. She stayed very close to his side—and he to hers—for the remainder of the party.

"I LOVE YOU, SPRING."

"I love you, too. Why didn't you tell me sooner?"

"I did. I told you Monday."

"But you haven't said it since."

"That's because I was waiting for you to say it."

Spring giggled. "God, we sound like teenagers."

He moved sinuously on top of her, bare skin sliding against bare skin as they lay in her bed. "Funny, I don't feel like a teenager."

Her eyes darkened and grew heavy. "No. No, you certainly don't. Oh, Clay."

CLAY LAUGHED SOFTLY, the movement vibrating his damp chest below her cheek. She lifted her head and looked at him curiously, her body gradually recovering from their intense, mind-shattering lovemaking. "What's so funny?"

"I was just thinking that I finally understand why Derek kept threatening to break my arm every time I put it around Summer when he first fell in love with her. It really brings out the caveman in a guy to see his woman looking so cozy with another man."

Remembering Clay's possessive reaction to Roger, Spring smiled and shook her head. "Derek's gotten over those jealous urges. You will, too."

"I suppose. But I still don't like other guys kissing you," he warned her semiseriously. "Especially old boyfriends."

"Now you know how I felt when Jessica started checking out the fit of your tight pants at Connie's party."

That piqued his interest. "Is that right?"

"I wanted to scratch her eyes out. And that's the first time in my life I ever wanted to do physical injury to another person. Other than you, of course."

"Of course." He cuddled her closer, his hand making lazy circles on her back. "These feelings between men and women are very complicated, aren't they? Overwhelming. Even scary sometimes."

"You're the psychologist. You should understand them," she replied, trying to keep the conversation light.

He shook his head. "It's different reading cases in books and actually experiencing the situations oneself. A few months ago I would have said that jealousy was counterproductive and unhealthy, that rational, clear-thinking adults did not waste time indulging in such negative emotions. I still believe that, and yet I wanted to rip off Roger's lips when they touched your face. So much for all that training."

"You're human, Clay. You managed to overcome your impulse and behave quite properly. You even had a very nice conversation with Roger before we left tonight."

"Well, he's not such a bad guy. A little dull, maybe, but Cathy will liven him up a bit. He wouldn't have been right for you, Spring."

"I know, darling. You're the one who's right for me. Exactly right for me."

"I love you."

"I love you, Clay."

He twisted until he was leaning over her. "Feel up to showing me again? I find myself still in need of reassurance."

She opened her arms to him, eager to find her own reassurance in his arms. Their future was still uncertain, but at least she knew now that he did love her. Surely their love could overcome any other obstacles that might lie ahead for them.

"C'MON, SPRING. Rise and shine. We're wasting sightseeing time."

Spring opened one eye, looked at the clock, noted that it was just seven in the morning and closed the eye with a loud groan. "Go away."

"No, really, sweetheart. By the time you shower and we have breakfast, it will be eight. You told me that it takes about forty minutes to get to Hot Springs, which will make it almost nine o'clock. We'll do some of the outdoor sights this morning before it gets too hot— God, it gets hot in Arkansas in July!—then we'll do indoor things until it cools off a bit. Museums, bathhouse tours, and so on. Spring, are you listening?"

"I'm sleeping."

"Don't make me have to tickle you, my love."

She opened that eye again, looking warily at him. "You wouldn't."

He held his hand over her bare side, fingers wiggling in mock threat. "Wouldn't I?"

She sighed and rolled over. "You win. I'll get up. Oh, God, you even look like a tourist. All you need is a camera slung around your neck."

"It's waiting in the living room," he replied happily, glancing down at his green T-shirt emblazoned with the words Arkansas Is A Natural, his khaki hiking shorts and his white tennis shoes.

"How come when I made my first visit to California, all I did was shop and visit my sister, and you come to Arkansas and try to memorize the state?"

"You just haven't learned the fine art of touristry," he answered with a grin. "Up, up, up. I'll be studying the history of the hot springs while you're showering. Did you know that they were used in healing rituals by the Indians and that Al Capone and Bugsy Siegel used to take the baths there on a regular basis?"

"No, but I'm sure I'll know all that and more by the end of the weekend." Spring climbed out of bed and brushed her hair out of her face, yawning. After getting so little sleep during their particularly active night, she was having a hard time keeping up with her exuberant lover. Not that she minded. She thought he was cute when he was in tourist mode.

She hummed in the shower, taking her time despite Clay's schedule. She intended to enjoy every moment of the weekend with him. Dressed in white shorts and a lemon-yellow top, she tossed a few things into an overnight bag and was ready for the weekend. All she had to do was drop Missy off with Mrs. English, who'd taken care of the cat while Spring was in California and was very fond of the pet.

Still humming softly, she went off in search of Clay. She found him in the living room, talking on the telephone. She paused in the doorway, realizing that he hadn't heard her approach. She didn't intend to eavesdrop, but she didn't want to disturb him, so she stood quietly for a moment, thinking he would notice her at any time.

"Okay, Frank," he was saying, his back still turned to her. "Gather it all up and hang on to it for me. I'll look it over when I get back. When? Oh, the week after next. Monday or Tuesday, at the latest. Yeah, I'm having fun. See you in a week, Frank."

Spring was back in her room before he'd cradled the receiver, her hand pressed to her stomach as if that would help the pain. She hadn't expected to hear him calmly making plans to return to California. He hadn't said a word to her about it. Sure, he'd told her when he'd arrived that he was here for a couple of weeks, but that had been before he'd told her that he loved her.

She'd thought that he would ask her to go with him when he decided to leave.

Pacing blindly around the room, she stumbled, then picked up the stuffed bear that had gotten under her feet. Holding him cradled to her chest, she stood in one spot, rocking slightly as she tried to tell herself that she wasn't breaking into pieces.

Be realistic, Spring. You knew he was only here on vacation. It was ironic, she thought with bitter humor, that their relationship had begun with a vacation fling—hers—and seemed to be ending with a vacation fling—his. No wonder he hadn't wanted to talk about their future. He didn't foresee one. At least not together.

Maybe he would still ask her to go with him, she thought on a surge of hope. And then shook her head in answer to her own thoughts. No. He surely would have said something to her before calmly making plans to leave.

Maybe he wasn't planning to end their relationship when he left. Perhaps he envisioned a long-distance affair—phone calls, letters, an occasional vacation together in California or Arkansas. Of course she knew where that would lead. Heartbreak. She didn't want to be separated from him. She didn't want to lie alone at night wondering whom he was with, what he was doing. She wanted to be his wife. She wanted to have his children. She wanted him!

"I'm having fun," he'd told Frank. *Fun?* He considered a full-scale love affair fun? Fine. She'd keep it that way for him. She'd told him goodbye before; she could do it again. She could live with a functioning machine where her heart was now. Because he would surely take her heart with him when he left.

It hurt. It hurt so much. But she wouldn't let him know. She refused to part badly with him again. She had him for another week, and she intended to create a lot of memories with him during that time. She would need them later.

"Spring, aren't you ready yet? Oh, there you are." Clay paused in the doorway and eyed her quizzically. "You planning to take the bear? It's fine with me, but I don't know if he's up to all the walking I plan to do. He looks kind of old."

She straightened her shoulders and forced a smile, setting Pooh back in his new spot on her bedroom floor. "I was just telling him to behave himself while we're gone. Is breakfast ready?"

"Yep. You have a choice of Raisin Bran and toast or Frosted Mini Wheats and toast."

"I'll have the Mini Wheats." She started past him, only to be stopped by his hand on her arm.

"Spring, are you all right?" he asked her, intently searching her face. "You look kind of funny."

She lifted an eyebrow. "Did you just call me funny looking?" she asked him in teasing challenge, hoping her smile would fool him.

He chuckled. "Of course not. I just wondered if anything was bothering you."

"I'm always like this when I'm roused from my bed at dawn after a strenuous night to face a breakfast of cold cereal and toast," she assured him airily. "To be followed by a long weekend of sight-seeing with the quintessential tourist."

"We're going to have a great time today," he assured her, looping his arm around her neck. "Trust me."

Trust him? The man who could—and probably would—break her heart? Okay, she'd trust him. For one more week, anyway.

"I love you, Spring," he murmured as they entered the kitchen.

"I love you, too, Clay." She was quite proud that she adequately hid the fact that her heart had already started to break as she spoke.

DURING THE WEEKEND Spring discovered that she was actually grateful for Clay's fascination with discovering new sights. He kept her much too busy to worry about the following week. They walked and played, climbed and explored, dined and danced until they were both barely able to crawl into bed Saturday evening, too tired even to make love. Though she'd expected to have a perfectly miserable day, she had a wonderful time, finding the fortitude somehow to push her problems to the back of her mind. She was with the man she loved; he was enjoying himself immensely. She couldn't be sad under those conditions. She even slept soundly and dreamlessly, waking to Clay's hand on her thigh, his mouth on her breast. She returned his lovemaking fiercely, determined to wring every ounce of satisfaction from her time with him.

"Spring, are you quite sure there's nothing wrong?" Clay asked her when he'd recovered part of his strength.

"I'm sure," she lied solemnly, kissing his shoulder.

He knew her too well to accept the words so easily, but he seemed to sense her wish for him to drop the subject. Perhaps he, too, wanted to make the most of the remaining week.

"In that case, let's get with it. I want to spend today at Magic Springs Amusement Park," he informed her breezily, climbing out of bed and heading for the shower.

Spring surreptitiously wiped away the tears she hadn't allowed him to see and ordered her mouth to smile. She decided that Summer wasn't the only Reed sister who'd been blessed with dramatic talent.

"Spring?"

"Okay, I'm hurrying," she assured her impatient lover, rushing to join him in the shower.

"SO WHAT'S CLAY DOING today? Memorizing the history of central Arkansas? Following the De Soto Trail along the Saline River through Benton? Counting the number of C-130 transport planes on the Little Rock Air Force Base in Jacksonville?" Kelsey grinned as she listed the possibilities on Tuesday afternoon in Spring's office.

Spring shook her head. "He's meeting with a local psychologist he read about in the paper last week. A man who works with troubled kids in their own homes. Clay called him yesterday and they talked for a long time, then set up this meeting for today."

"Got a real talent for meeting people, doesn't he? I couldn't believe how well he fit in at Gordon's on Friday. It was like he'd known the gang for years."

"Yes, he's very good with people." Spring completed a report, signed it and handed it to Kelsey. "There you go. All finished."

"Okay, I'll take care of it." Kelsey paused, frowning a bit, then asked carefully, "Is anything wrong, Spring?"

"No, why do you ask?" The lie was coming easier all the time.

"No reason. It's just that you've looked, I don't know, kind of sad since you came in yesterday morning after your weekend in Hot Springs. I hope you're not having problems with Clay. The two of you seem so good together."

"No, Kelsey, we're not having problems." And they weren't. They were getting along fine. But Clay still hadn't bothered to mention that he was leaving in only a few days. Her hope had slowly dwindled and finally fizzled out completely. If he'd been planning to ask her to marry him and move with him to California, he would surely have done so by now. He was leaving in less than a week.

And still she'd managed to hide her pain from him. She must be a much better actress than she'd ever suspected.

CLAY WAS on the telephone again when she walked into her apartment after work. Again she had the impression that he was talking to Frank. He saw her this time as soon as she entered the room, stopped whatever he was saying in midsentence, then went on with a few vague, general remarks that could mean anything before hanging up.

"Just checking on things in San Francisco," he explained.

"How are things in San Francisco?" Maybe now he would tell her his plans, she thought.

"Oh, just fine," he answered uninformatively. "Hey, did I tell you I heard from Thelma a couple of weeks ago?"

"No, you didn't. How is she?" He was putting her off again. Why?

"She's doing great. She's crazy about her aunt and she's being tutored this summer so that she'll be ready for tenth grade this fall. She's in music classes and she's made a couple of friends—and she assures me they're nice kids who won't lead her into more trouble. I've got a lot of hope for that kid."

"She owes a great deal to you, Clay."

He flushed unexpectedly and shrugged. "Just doing my job."

His job? He'd never made a penny from his work at Halloran House, where he'd met Thelma, and she knew it. She smiled at his modesty.

"You haven't even kissed me yet," Clay told her suddenly. "C'mere."

After the kiss her arms remained around him, tightening compulsively as she held him. She never wanted to let him go.

Clay returned the hug with enthusiasm, then held her away from him. "What did I do to deserve that?"

"I love you," she told him, unable to smile.

"I love you, too." He kissed her again, then laughed and turned her toward the kitchen, keeping his arm snugly around her waist. "Let's find something to eat before we get distracted and miss dinner again. I'm starving."

Slipping into the determinedly lighthearted mood that she was rapidly becoming an expert at assuming, she matched her steps to his. "How did your meeting with Dr. Random go today? Are you still intrigued by his new method?"

"Very much so. I had a few suggestions to make that he seemed to like, and we had an informal consultation on a couple of kids he's been treating lately—no names, of course. We managed to preserve his confidentiality. We're having lunch tomorrow."

She looked up at him in surprise. "You must really be interested in this man's work."

"Of course I am. It's the same work as mine," he answered logically, smiling as he released her to open the refrigerator door and peer hopefully inside.

He must be missing his work very much, Spring thought sadly, if he was spending so much time just talking about another man's job. He must be looking forward to getting home.

Oh, good, Spring. Why don't you twist the knife a little harder? she asked herself impatiently. Deciding abruptly to make some iced tea, she reached into the cabinet for tea bags, groaning when her sudden move bumped her elbow into the sugar bowl on the counter. Sugar spilled across the counter and onto the tile floor at her feet in a glistening white stream. "Damn."

Without pausing a beat Clay leaped into the puddle of sugar on the floor and began to do a soft-shoe routine, whistling "Tea for Two" as he slid the toe of his sneaker through the white powder. Spring had to laugh as she pulled out the broom and dustpan, shaking her head at his antics. God, she was going to miss him!

KELSEY ACTED ODDLY on Thursday. Spring asked twice if her friend was ill or troubled about something, but Kelsey only looked mysterious and shook her dark head, her brown eyes twinkling with mischief. Even Andi kept eyeing Spring with a secretive smile that was making her decidedly nervous. What was going on, anyway?

She found out right after lunch. She'd just finished with a patient and walked out into the hallway to find Clay waiting for her. He grabbed her and kissed her, right in front of Kelsey and Andi, before she could speak.

When he released her, she frowned at the expressions on the three faces grinning at her. "What's going on? What are you doing here, Clay?"

"I'm kidnapping you for the afternoon," he informed her. "Get your purse."

She sighed. "Clay, I have appointments this afternoon. I can't just leave."

"Wrong," Andi told her. "You're quite free this afternoon."

"Are you crazy? I looked at the calendar this morning. The afternoon was booked."

"All the appointments have been rescheduled to the patients' satisfaction," Kelsey informed her smugly. "You're going to be working a few extra hours tomorrow and Monday to make up for it, but you're off for the rest of the day. Enjoy."

Spring narrowed her eyes at Clay, who was looking innocently back at her. He was wearing disreputable jeans and a Mickey Mouse T-shirt, and even the mouse looked blandly conspiratorial to her suspicious eyes. "Clay, what are you planning?"

"Sight-seeing," he told her succinctly. "Get your purse."

Groaning, she tugged off her white lab coat and got her purse.

"Well?" she asked him when they were in her car and on their way. "Where are we going?"

"I've found something really interesting. Ever heard of the Quapaw Quarter?"

"You're taking me to see the Quapaw Quarter?" she asked in bewilderment.

"Yes. It's an area of downtown Little Rock full of old homes ranging in architectural style from the pre-1836 Territorial Period to the 1940s. Many of them are Victorian mansions or large cottages, and some have been completely restored to their former magnificence. About five hundred homes and buildings in the six-square-mile area have been renovated or fixed up, with a total investment of some twenty million dollars. There are—"

"Clay!" Spring loudly interrupted. What *was* going on? Clay always liked to talk, but now he was positively chattering!

"Yes?"

"What are you quoting?"

He looked sheepish. "A publication that I picked up from the Quapaw Quarter Association. Did you know that there are a thousand members of the Quapaw Quarter Associ—"

"Clay, I know about the Quapaw Quarter. They have tours of some of the restored old homes every Christmas and every spring, which I've been on several times. *This* is why you kidnapped me from my office?"

"Just wait, Spring," he told her mysteriously.

Thoroughly confused, she leaned back against her seat and waited, noting in surprise that he was holding the steering wheel in a white-knuckled grip.

Clay drove slowly down Broadway, pointing out some of the restored homes, such as the Bankston House, the Thompson House and the Foster-Robinson House. He turned on Twenty-first, taking them over to Spring Street, a name he pointed out gleefully.

"I was well aware it was here," Spring told him, but he ignored her, chatting away like a tour guide to a true foreigner. She frowned when he pulled into the drive of a gray frame Victorian cottage on Spring Street. "Why are you stopping?"

He dangled a key in front of her, his eyes not quite meeting hers. "Private tour."

"We're going inside?"

"Yep. The realtor is holding my Rolex, all my credit cards and my firstborn child hostage until I return the key."

"Why?"

"So I won't take the key and run, I guess. I thought it was kind of silly. After all, the key's not worth that much, and it would be pretty hard to steal the house—"

"Clay, why are we going into this house?" she asked, holding on to her patience with an effort.

"You and I are both interested in restoring old homes, and this one is really nice. Restoration was begun a couple of years ago. Then the couple who'd started had to sell and move away, so nothing much has been done since, but it has a lot of potential. Wait until you see the gingerbread trim inside. Wonderful!"

Her heart had started to pound, but she told herself not to read too much into this odd private tour. For all she knew, Clay could just be sight-seeing, as he'd told her.

He kept up a running commentary as he led her onto the front porch, with its quaintly delicate columns, and to the door, a heavy wooden one with a lead-glass fanlight above it. "This house and most of the others in the Quarter have been researched and the information kept on file by the QQA, the Quapaw Quarter Association. They also keep a library of books on the art of restoration and preservation of historic houses, hoping to encourage more people to take on these homes as family projects."

Though part of her mind followed his words, another part of her noted in growing fascination that there was a nervous edge to his voice and that his hand was shaking so hard he had trouble fitting the key into the lock. Her own hands began to tremble. In fact, she was trembling all over as she followed him inside.

"Look at that staircase. Isn't it fantastic? And these floors. They need sanding and refinishing, of course, but they're—"

His voice broke. Shoving his shaking hands into the pockets of his jeans, he went still, staring at her with eyes that were shadowed by deep emotion.

"Clay?" she whispered, unable to look away from his face to notice any of the features of the house. "What is it?"

He took a deep breath and looked down at his sneakers. "Did you ever want something so very much that you thought you'd die if you didn't get it? Want it so much that you were afraid to even ask for it for fear of being turned down?"

"Yes," she answered, her voice raw. "Yes, I've wanted that much." *You, Clay. I want you that much. And I'm so afraid to hope.*

"I need you so much, Spring." He shot her a quick glance, looked away, then slowly turned his eyes back to her. "All my life I've wanted to be loved. The kids love me and my friends love me, and for the past few years I've thought that was enough. Until I met you. I almost died after you left, Spring. For four long months I lived in misery, so lonely that I felt like there was a gaping hole inside me. It scared me to realize that you were the only one who could fill that void. And I resented you for a while for making me need like that again, after considering myself satisfied for so long."

"Clay, I—"

"No, wait, sweetheart, let me finish." He laughed, a bit weakly, and shrugged. "I've been practicing this speech for a long time."

She nodded and blinked against a sudden rush of tears as he continued.

"I didn't want to say anything right away because I wanted you to get used to having me around all the time. In California there were always other people with us or around us, but here it's been pretty much just the two of us. I thought you'd know by now whether you wanted to have me around full-time. And I've been checking out Little Rock and the surrounding area because I wasn't sure at first if I'd be happy here, but now I know that it's a great place to live and . . . and raise a family."

His voice had cracked again, sending the tears in a fresh cascade down Spring's pale cheeks. She had to bite her lower lip to keep from interrupting him before he was finished.

"There are some excellent counseling facilities for adolescents here, most of which I visited last week. And Gil—Dr. Random—has asked if I might be interested in going into partnership with him. He seems to think that the two of us could make a real difference around here, maybe publish some material that could be applied nationwide. I told him I would certainly think about it. I have to admit I'm tempted to take him up on it.

"We wouldn't have to live here, of course. Your apartment is very nice, or there are many beautiful newer homes in west Little Rock, closer to your office than this. I'd be happy anywhere if you were there with me."

He took one more deep breath, then blurted out, "What I'm trying to say, Spring, is . . . will you marry me? Please say you will, Spring."

"Yes," she whispered, and then said it again, louder, throwing herself against him. "Yes, yes, yes!"

Staggering, he caught her and spun her around in a joyous circle. "You will? Oh, God, Spring, you don't know how happy you've just made me!"

Laughing and crying all at once, she cupped his face between her hands and kissed him. "How could you possibly be so surprised? Didn't you know I would marry you?"

"Oh, sweetheart, I'm not that self-confident. Ever since last weekend you've been acting a bit distracted and I was starting to get scared that you were growing tired of me. That you were ready for me to go back to San Francisco and let you get back to your sane, normal life."

"You idiot," she told him lovingly. "I was distracted because *I* was scared. I heard you talking to Frank on Saturday about returning home in about a week, and I was afraid that you were planning to leave without me."

He laughed softly and held her close. "God, we're so insecure when it comes to each other. That's exactly the way I reacted four months ago when I thought you were calmly making plans to return to Little Rock without a backward look at me. It's going to take a legal, binding, double-ring ceremony for me to get over my fear of losing you, Spring. When will you marry me?"

"Whenever you want," she answered simply. "And you don't have to live in Arkansas if you really don't want to, Clay. I decided four months ago that I would move to San Francisco if you wanted me to."

"You'd be willing to give up your friends, the practice that you've worked so hard to build?" he asked, seemingly stunned by her offer.

"Of course. Aren't you offering to do the same thing for me?"

He kissed her thoroughly, then drew back to smile down at her. "Thank you. But I like it here. I'm perfectly happy to move. It'll take me some time to get everything settled, but most of it can be done long-distance. I've already been talking to Frank about setting up a foundation for long-range money management so that Halloran House can be run without my day-to-day help, or interference, as some people might call it. And I can sell my house easily enough."

"Don't sell it yet," Spring urged him suddenly, her fingers gripping his T-shirt. "Lease it for a year."

He frowned, puzzled. "Why?"

"Because I want you to be very sure when you do sever that connection to San Francisco. If, at the end of a year, you're not as happy here as you were in California, I want you to tell me. We'll move—there, or anywhere else you want to go. As long as we're together, I don't care where we live."

"That's not necessary, darling. I know what I'm doing."

"Please, Clay. For me."

"All right, Spring. I'll lease the house. But at the end of one year I'll be selling it. I've found my home here, with you."

"I love you, Clay."

"I love you," he murmured against her lips, and then his mouth took hers in newly confirmed possession, his tongue touching hers in a mating dance that made the upcoming ceremony a mere formality. In their minds and hearts they had already made their lifetime commitment to each other.

His body growing taut with desire, Clay smiled down at her with an expression she recognized, her body responding quite physically to the silent invitation. "I haven't shown you around the house yet, have I? Particularly the bedroom."

"No, you haven't. Show me our house, Clay."

"Our house? You like it?"

"I love it. I can't wait to put on jeans and a work shirt and start remodeling with you. How are you at hanging wallpaper?"

"I'm hell on wheels at wallpaper. It's going to be a lot of work, Spring."

"It's something I've always wanted to do. I even have my own set of tools, thanks to my sister Autumn."

He had to stop to hug her again. "You are terrific, did you know that?"

"I'm perfectly willing to be convinced."

"Oh, I intend to convince you, darling. If it takes a lifetime."

"I suspect that it will."

There was another surprise waiting for her in the large, almost completely renovated master bedroom. In front of the native-stone fireplace—a mate to the one in the living room—a handmade quilt had been spread invitingly. A silver ice bucket held a bottle of champagne, and two crystal glasses with beribboned stems waited for a toast. A dozen red roses in a tall crystal vase perfumed the room, masking the faint dustiness of the empty house.

"Oh, Clay." She turned to him, her eyes filling again at the blatant sentimentality of his gesture. "What would you have done if I'd said no?"

"Poured the champagne over your head, thrown you onto the quilt and made love to you until you were too weak to argue with me," he returned promptly, holding out his hand. "Come here, sweetheart. Let's toast our very brief engagement."

"How brief?" she asked with interest, placing her hand in his and allowing him to lead her across the room and seat her on the quilt.

"As brief as your practice and my settling of affairs will allow," he replied, popping the cork and pouring two bubbling glasses of champagne. "To a long and happy life together, my love."

She touched her glass to his and lifted it to her lips, unable even to taste the expensive wine in her excitement and joy.

Clay took only one swallow from his glass, equally oblivious to the taste, his gaze fastened on the flushed, happy face of his future wife. His nerves, which had been tight with anxiety earlier, began to thrum with another type of anticipation. Still having trouble believing in his good fortune, he wanted to further seal their commitment in the most basic manner of all. He wanted to make love to her, to bury himself deep inside her and remind himself over and over that he had every right to be there, that she was his and he was hers and he would never be lonely again.

Her eyes met his, and he watched her read the message he was sending her, watched her eyelids grow heavy, her lips soften and glisten as she moistened them with just the tip of her tongue. A groan started deep in his chest and forced its way through his throat. He set his drink down abruptly and reached for her, barely giving her time to set her own glass safely out of the way.

And then he was kissing her and holding her, and she was holding him, loving him, needing him, filling that lifelong void inside him. Filling it so perfectly that it would never open again. And because he'd craved that feeling for so long, he felt his eyes filling with tears of happiness and gratitude. Spring kissed away his tears, even as he did hers, and then sweetness turned to passion and tenderness to hunger and they were tossing aside clothes and reaching for each other. His thrust took him deep, deep inside her, and her arch forced him even deeper until neither of them could tell where one left off and the other began. They were one, and they would have settled for nothing less.

The words he muttered into her ear as he rocked against her, inside her, were disjointed and not particularly clever, punctuated by ragged gasps and broken sighs, but she knew what he was telling her and her clenched hands and sinuous movements answered him in kind. By the time they shuddered together and cried out their fulfillment, there was no further doubt of their love or commitment.

It seemed like a very long time later when Spring stirred, sighed and lifted her head to smile at Clay. "I hope no one else decides to check out this house in the next few minutes," she told him, lying nude alongside him on the rumpled blanket.

He chuckled. "Good point. Though the realtor assured me that I had the only key, I guess there's no need to press our luck. Maybe we should get dressed."

"I love this bedroom." She looked around the room with pleasure, anticipating many happy times there with Clay.

"There are two other bedrooms you haven't seen yet. Think we can come up with a use for them?" Clay asked hopefully.

"I'm sure we'll think of something," she answered, picturing two blond children with blue-green eyes and beautiful smiles and unusual taste in clothing.

"Someone once told me that I'll be better with kids once I've had some of my own."

She winced as she remembered their quarrel. "That someone sounds like an idiot. You're already great with kids."

"I'd still like to have a family with you. A boy and a girl. Or two boys. Or two girls. Or three or four of each."

She laughed and shook her head firmly. "Two sounds like plenty."

"Just think—we can all wear matching outfits!"

She groaned and hid her face in his shoulder. By the time she came up for air, he had grown serious, looking steadily at her, as he spoke. "I'm not going to be all that easy to live with, Spring. I get so wrapped up in young people's problems sometimes that I tend to ignore everything else, and I can't promise you that won't ever happen with you. It's a part of me that I can't seem to change, and I don't know that I even want to try."

"I don't want you to change, Clay. I love you exactly the way you are. You are a caring, loving, sensitive man, and your concern for young people is one of the reasons I fell in love with you. I care about them, too. I'd like to help you, if I can. I won't feel neglected if I'm involved, too."

"That sounds wonderful," he told her with a smile. "I promise, though, that I'll always be there for you and our children when you need me. All you have to do is ask and I'll drop everything else. Got that?"

"Got it. And I believe you, darling. You're already giving up so much to move here to be with me."

"I'm not giving up a fraction as much as I'm gaining," he returned firmly. "Remember that, will you?"

"Just keep reminding me, darling." She gave him a brilliant smile as she reached for her clothes.

"I intend to." He reached out and caught her hand, tugging her back down in a sprawl across his chest. "Believe me, sweetheart. I intend to."

Epilogue

HER MOTHER'S antique lace gown fell in soft folds to strike Spring at midcalf—it had fallen almost to Summer's ankles when Summer had worn it for her wedding ten months earlier. Fortunately, the sisters were almost the same size except in height, so the dress hadn't needed altering. A white hat and her grandmother's pearl earrings—returned to her earlier that day by Kelsey—completed her wedding outfit. Spring checked her appearance one last time in the full-length mirror in the bedroom that had been hers while growing up. In only a few minutes her wedding would begin.

As Spring had wished, it was to be a relatively small, informal affair on her mother's beautifully kept, flower-decorated back lawn. They'd waited until early evening so that the August heat would have dissipated a bit, though it was still very warm. Her parents, relatives and close friends—some fifty people in all—would make up the audience. Summer and Autumn were to serve as bridesmaids, while Derek and Dr. Gil Random, Clay's new partner, would stand beside the groom.

"Are you nervous, honey?" Lila Reed asked softly, faded violet eyes focused on her eldest daughter's serene face.

"A little. But I don't have one doubt that I'm doing the right thing," Spring assured her mother. "Clay is the best thing that ever happened to me, Mom."

"Just be happy, Spring." Lila hugged her daughter, then stepped back, surreptitiously wiping her eyes.

"I will be." Spring picked up the bouquet of colorful flowers that Clay had provided for her—a beautiful but unusual mixture, of course—and turned toward the door. "I'm ready. Is Daddy waiting in the hall?"

"Yes, and he's ready to get this over with. He's just as nervous this time as he was when he gave Summer away."

"Tell him to take heart. Autumn swears she'll never go through this 'archaic and obsolete ceremony,' so maybe this will be his last time."

"Autumn's young yet. We'll see how she feels when she meets someone as special as your Clay and Summer's Derek."

"Speaking of my Clay, what *is* he wearing, Mom? I can't stand the suspense." Spring had cheerfully given Clay free rein to wear whatever he wanted to their wedding, but he had refused to tell her what he'd chosen. She hadn't seen him since he'd gone off to change for the ceremony an hour earlier.

Lila shook her gray head, smiling girlishly. "He made me promise that I wouldn't tell you. That boy is sure going to liven up our lives, honey. I'm glad ya'll decided to settle in Little Rock so your dad and I can see you often."

"So am I, Mom. Okay, let's get on with this."

Her hand tucked into the crook of her father's work-muscled arm, the fabric of his favorite brown suit crisp under her fingers, Spring walked down the aisle formed by rows of folding metal chairs, her eyes sparkling with happiness and amusement. Flanked by Autumn and

Summer in their jewel-toned summery dresses and Derek and Gil in their conservative suits, Clay fit in surprisingly well. His suit was dark blue, hand tailored, European cut. His shirt was white, his tie a muted stripe. He looked as breathtakingly handsome in his conservative attire as he did in tropical-print shorts. Spring's heart swelled with love for him.

He stepped forward to meet her, catching her hand in his as his eyes glowed warmly into hers.

"A blue suit, Clay?" she murmured.

"In honor of this serious occasion, my love," he replied softly.

"Clay, I told you that I didn't want you to change for me. I love you exactly the way you are."

He stared down at her for a moment, then gave her a smile that competed with the August sun in intensity. "I love you, Spring," he murmured, then caught her to him for a long, passionate kiss, much to the amusement of their small audience.

"You're supposed to wait until *after* the ceremony, Clay," Derek pointed out from his position as best man.

Clay chuckled and released her, though he directed her attention downward as he lifted the hem of his beautifully cut pants. "I haven't changed, Spring. I'm still the man who loves you more than life itself. Just wait until you see what I have on under the suit."

Glancing at his bare ankles, Spring smiled and turned with him toward the perplexed minister, toward their future. The next time Clay kissed her, they were husband and wife.

GIFTS FROM THE HEART
MAIL-IN-OFFER
OFFER CERTIFICATE

I have enclosed the required number of proofs of purchase from any specially marked "Gifts From The Heart" Harlequin romance book, plus cash register receipts and a check or money order payable to Harlequin Gifts From The Heart Offer, to cover postage and handling.

002

CHECK ONE	ITEM	# OF PROOFS OF PURCHASE	POSTAGE & HANDLING FEE
	01 Brass Picture Frame	2	$ 1.00
	02 Heart-Shaped Candle Holders with Candles	3	$ 1.00
	03 Heart-Shaped Keepsake Box	4	$ 1.00
	04 Gold-Plated Heart Pendant	5	$ 1.00
	05 Collectors' Doll Limited quantities available	12	$ 2.75

NAME _____

STREET ADDRESS _____ APT. # _____

CITY _____ STATE _____ ZIP _____

Mail this certificate, designated number of proofs of purchase (inside back page) and check or money order for postage and handling to:

Gifts From The Heart, P.O. Box 4814
Reidsville, N. Carolina 27322-4814

NOTE THIS IMPORTANT OFFER'S TERMS

Requests must be postmarked by May 31, 1988. Only proofs of purchase from specially marked "Gifts From The Heart" Harlequin books will be accepted. This certificate plus cash register receipts and a check or money order to cover postage and handling must accompany your request and may not be reproduced in any manner. Offer void where prohibited, taxed or restricted by law. LIMIT ONE REQUEST PER NAME, FAMILY, GROUP, ORGANIZATION OR ADDRESS. Please allow up to 8 weeks after receipt of order for shipment. Offer only good in the U.S.A. Hurry—Limited quantities of collectors' doll available. Collectors' dolls will be mailed to first 15,000 qualifying submitters. All other submitters will receive 12 free previously unpublished Harlequin books and a postage & handling refund.

OFFER-1RR

HARLEQUIN *Temptation*

SUMMER REED WAS HOLDING OUT FOR A HERO... AND SHE FOUND HIM!

In Temptation #174, Summer discovered an irresistible *Hero in Disguise*. In Temptations #198 and #204, you'll meet her two sisters and *their* heroes.

This month we bring you a *Hero for the Asking*. A rather straitlaced optometrist named Spring encounters mesmerizing, unorthodox Clay McEntire, who only has eyes for her.

Next month, *Hero by Nature* will captivate you. When pediatrician Jeff Bradford hires Autumn, a feisty, red-haired electrician to fix his wiring, the sparks fly....

Enjoy these two sizzlers from Gina Wilkins, one of Temptation's hottest new authors.

T198-1R

GIFTS FROM THE HEART

from *Harlequin*

FREE BY MAIL With proofs of purchase
plus postage and handling

A. **Hand-polished solid brass picture frame 1-5/8″ × 1-3/8″ with 2 proofs of purchase.**

B. **Individually handworked, pair of heart-shaped glass candle holders (2″ diameter), 6″ candles included, with 3 proofs of purchase.**

C. **Heart-shaped porcelain keepsake box (1″ high) with delicate flower motif with 4 proofs of purchase.**

D. **Radiant gold-plated heart pendant on 16″ chain with complimentary satin pouch with 5 proofs of purchase.**

E. **Beautiful collectors' doll with genuine porcelain face, hands and feet, and a charming heart appliqué on dress with 12 proofs of purchase. Limited quantities available. See offer terms.**

HERE IS HOW TO GET YOUR FREE GIFTS

Send us the required number of proofs of purchase (below) of specially marked "Gifts From The Heart" Harlequin books and cash register receipts with the Offer Certificate (available in the back pages) properly completed, plus a check or money order (do not send cash) payable to Harlequin Gifts From The Heart Offer. We'll RUSH you your specified gift. Hurry—Limited quantities of collectors' doll available. See offer terms.

GIFTS FROM THE HEART

303R

ONE PROOF
OF PURCHASE

To collect your free gift by mail you must include the necessary number of proofs of purchase with order certificate.